tim bowler

BLADE

FIGHTING BACK

Blade is back in the Beast, the city he fled from at the age of eleven, the place he hates and fears. But there's no avoiding it now. The grinks have taken Jaz, the little girl who has become the centre of his life, and he knows they've brought her here.

But the Beast is even more dangerous than the last city. Enemies lurk in every shadow and the police are hunting him too. Blade will only have one chance to rescue Jaz and it will take all his nerve and skill. It's time to fight back, before it's too late . . .

The fifth title in this ground-breaking series from Tim Bowler, the Carnegie Medal-winning author of *River Boy*, *Starseeker*, *Frozen Fire* and *Bloodchild*. The tension is greater than ever as Blade prepares to face his deadliest enemy of all . . .

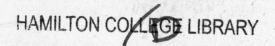

Other Books by Tim Bowler

tim bowler

winner of the carnegie medal

BLADE

FIGHTING BACK

book 5

OXFORD

UNIVERSITY PRESS

OXFORD
UNIVERSITY PRESS

Great Clarendon Street, Oxford OX2 6DP

Oxford University Press is a department of the University of Oxford.
It furthers the University's objective of excellence in research, scholarship,
and education by publishing worldwide in

Oxford   New York

Auckland   Cape Town   Dar es Salaam   Hong Kong   Karachi
Kuala Lumpur   Madrid   Melbourne   Mexico City   Nairobi
New Delhi   Shanghai   Taipei   Toronto

With offices in

Argentina   Austria   Brazil   Chile   Czech Republic   France   Greece
Guatemala   Hungary   Italy   Japan   Poland   Portugal   Singapore
South Korea   Switzerland   Thailand   Turkey   Ukraine   Vietnam

Oxford is a registered trade mark of Oxford University Press
in the UK and in certain other countries

British Library Cataloguing in Publication Data

Data available

ISBN: 978-0-19-275598-8

1 3 5 7 9 10 8 6 4 2

Printed in Great Britain by CPI Cox and Wyman, Reading, Berkshire

Paper used in the production of this book is a natural,
recyclable product made from wood grown in sustainable forests.
The manufacturing process conforms to the environmental
regulations of the country of origin.

For Rachel,
with my love

Welcome to the Big Beast. Welcome to Hell.

Check around you, Bigeyes. Early morning, November sun. Cute little street, cute little school, cute little kiddies trigging through the gate. The great capital waking up around us. Plum place, yeah?

Think again.

Cos it's all wrong. It's zipping you over. Everything you see, everything you feel. Come closer, Bigeyes, and listen good. This is big new grime. It's not like the old city, the one we just escaped from.

1

BLADE

This is the Beast.

And I'll tell you something about him.

Something you got to know.

Makes no difference how much sun there is, how many dinky kids or spiced up people you can see waking and shaking their lives into gear. The Beast's not what you think. Not what anyone thinks.

I know what I'm talking about. I was born here. I grew up here. If you can call it growing up. But never mind that. I know the Beast, right? I know him like I know my own body. If you think I was brained up on the old city, that's nothing to what I know about the Beast.

You probably heard about the taxi drivers. How they know every single street in the city. They learn it, road by road, and they get tested on it. Like it's a qualification. Yeah, right. Is that meant to impress me?

Well, it doesn't. I knew all that gump by the time I was seven. Every lane, every street, every dronky little mews. All the places too. Hotels, clubs, theatres, cinemas, brothels, you name it. All the bollocky monuments. I got so bored knowing everything about the Beast I made up my own names for all the different places.

I got that kind of memory. I remember everything I want to remember. People, places, stories, numbers, whatever. You wouldn't believe the stuff I can remember. That's one of the things that's got me in trouble. But here's what's weird about the Beast.

I learnt all these things about him, then I found I was wrong. I didn't really know the Beast at all. Not like I thought I did. I just knew the names, and the places to hide. I know him better now. You bet I do. And you got to get cracked on him too, Bigeyes.

Cos there's stuff about the Beast you got to learn fast.

First up, he's not like the old city. The one we just left. She was big, yeah, but she's nothing to this guy. Second, the Beast's not even a city, not even a capital. Yeah, yeah, he's called both. In the tourist books.

He's got all the bung they blab about. Stations, parks, banks, businesses, stores, sights, all that shit. But he's got something else too. Something you won't find in the tourist books.

Another city.

And another, and another, and another.

Cos here's what most nebs don't know. We're not

in a city. We're in ten cities rolled into one. More than ten. The Beast's a country all his own. And I'm not just talking about size, Bigeyes, how far he spreads out. I'm talking about layers. Cities within cities, lives within lives.

That's where the darkness comes from.

The cities you don't see.

The lives you don't see.

Trust me. I know.

But never mind that now. Cop a glint over the kids. Most of 'em in the playground but some still ripping in through the gate. Keep back, well back, and watch cute. Stay behind this van and peep round the edge.

OK, Bigeyes, got the kids? Got the main gate? Right, now check out the car parked down on the left, the flash grey one. And the guy sitting at the wheel. Smooth gobbo, shiny suit, sharp eyes.

See 'em moving? Can't, can you? That's cos he's cute and you're a dimp. Look again, Bigeyes. Look better. Got 'em now? The eyes? Still missing 'em, aren't you? Dungpot.

Never mind. Take it from me. They're moving. I know. How do I know? Cos he's like me. He knows how to watch. So we got to stay fizzed. For one very good reason.

The bastards know I'm here.

Back at the Beast, I mean. I'm not talking about this little street, or this gobbo. Jesus, if he knew what's going on, I might as well flip over now. But he doesn't. He's smart and he watches good, but he hasn't slammed me. And he won't, unless I dunk it big time.

He's like all the other grinks. Does what he's told, gets paid, goes home. Asks no questions. No, I'm not talking about him. I'm talking about the scumbos who tell him what to do, and the slimeheads above them. They're the ones who'll know I'm back at the Beast.

It's a simple equation.

They got Jaz and they know I'll come for her. Cos they know I care. Xennie slung that one when she blotched on me and Bex. So they'll know I won't wig it out of here and all they got to do is wait till I show.

And they're right. I've come back for Jaz. She's all I want. I don't give two bells what happens to me long as she gets away safe. But I'll tell you something, Bigeyes. If she's dead, there's something else I'll have.

My revenge.

That's right, Bigeyes.

I'm fighting back.

Only problem is what to do about Bex. I can't leave her and she's clogged onto me. She's still mad at me. When the police turned up at the old prof's house, she was splitting my ear so bad we nearly didn't get away.

But I got her down the stairs and out the back door, and we made it over the fields to the motorway. Don't ask me how we didn't get caught. It's been a day and a night of hitching and hiding.

But here we are.

Still together. She's locked onto me, Bigeyes, and I can't drop her. She wants Jaz back as bad as I do. Problem is, I work better on my own. If Bex chokes up—which she could do easy—she'll shunt us both.

Check over my shoulder.

No sign of her, thank Christ. Been blamming my head over the thought of her standing in the middle of the road, tramping my gig for everyone to see. Took all my licky to persuade her to stay out of sight while I sniff out this patch.

But she's done it. Can't say she hasn't. Just hope she's where I left her. Cos there's no betting she will be. OK, we better shift before those gobbos clap us.

Yeah, Bigeyes, you heard right. I said gobbos. Didn't see the second guy, did you? Over to the right, further down. Got him now? Beefcake, grey suit, leaning against the outside wall of the playground.

Let's get out of here.

Back down the street, keeping behind the parked cars. Check about you, Bigeyes, check good. Cos everywhere we go now, we got to keep out of sight and watch cute. We got to see the shit before the shit sees us.

There's more dangers in the Beast than in the old city. She was bad but this bastard's got eyes everywhere. Down to the bottom of the street, check round, check again, through the park, past the tube, into the alleyway.

Stop, check the street behind. All clear. Down the alleyway, follow the bend round, up to the wall at the end.

And there's Bex.

Slumped on the ground behind the big dustbin. Just where I left her. I breathe slowly out. Thought she might have wigged it. And that'd be bad, Bigeyes. The grinks'd chew her up in five minutes if she cut off on her own.

She looks up, accusing.

'Didn't think you'd come back,' she sulks.

'I told you I would.'

'Yeah.' She sniffs. 'You done.'

'Meaning what?'

'Meaning your word ain't worth shit.'

'I've stuck with you. All the way here. I could have cleared off any time I wanted.'

'Whatever.'

She looks away, looks back.

'Ain't only me, is it?' she gripes. 'Not trusting.'

'I don't know what you're talking about.'

I do, Bigeyes. But never mind that.

'You don't trust me neither,' she goes on. 'I can see it in your face. I watched you coming down the alleyway. You was thinking I bet that slag's pissed off.'

'I don't think you're a slag.'

'But you was thinking I'd pissed off.'

I shrug.

'Whatever.'

She bursts into tears. First time she's blubbed since we scraped it out the old prof's house. She was all tears in there, and I don't blame her. Dig murdered, Jaz taken, all the grime. But since we got away she's gone quiet. She's still blazing at me—I can feel that—but it's from the inside. Like a weird, silent anger. No words, no frowns, no punches or slaps.

And no tears.

Till now. But maybe that's best. She's got a lot of stuff inside her.

Like me.

Only difference is I'm not crying. And you know why, Bigeyes? Cos I won't let myself. I've told myself no tears till I get Jaz back. I got to be strong for that kid.

Bex goes on blubbing.

I sit down next to her, let her bawl. She takes no notice of me. It's a few minutes before she's quiet again. Just sits there, wet eyes, half-open. She's gone into herself again. Then suddenly she turns her head, fixes me.

'You got to talk,' she says.

I look at her. She's not just angry now. She's close to breaking up. I can see it in her face. And there's something else, Bigeyes. She's right. I owe her some words.

And anyway, she needs to know a bit.

Not all of it. Not sure I can tell all of it. But some of it. If only so she knows how dangerous things are. But I guess she's clapped that already.

'That guy in the house,' she mutters. 'The one what said tell Blade if he wants the little girl back, he knows where to come.'

'What about him?'

'Was he right?'

'Maybe.'

'Maybe?' She grabs me by the collar, thrusts her face close. 'Maybe?'

'Bex—'

'Was he right, yes or no?'

'He was right.'

'You shit!'

She pushes me away.

'Bex—'

'Shut it!'

'Bex—'

'I said shut it!'

I'm thinking hard, Bigeyes. How to do this. She wants me to talk but she's too angry to listen. I got to get her back on my side or we're spiked. I jump up, reach out a hand.

'Come here, Bex.'

She looks up at me like I got a disease.

'I don't need your frigging hand to get up.'

She climbs to her feet by herself. She's swaying, still bombed, still choked.

'So what you got for me now?' she grumps. 'More lies?'

'I want to show you something.'

I don't wait for her, just walk back down the alleyway. I can hear her following. More of a waddle than a walk but she's coming. Round the bend, on to the end of the alleyway, stop, check round into the street.

Looks cute. But I'm wary.

Bex catches up, stops by my shoulder.

'Where we going?' she mutters.

'Nowhere.'

'So what you wasting my time for?'

'Look over the road.'

She's quiet for a moment. I don't check if she's watching. I know she is. I can feel it.

'What's so special?' she says suddenly.

'Tell me what you see. Over the road.'

'Houses.'

'Look again. Left to right. Tell me what you see.'

She gives a sigh.

'Go on,' I say.

'House, house, house, house,' she goes, bored voice, 'house, empty space, house—'

'Stop.'

'What?'

'Look at the empty space.'

Another silence. Again I don't check. Again I feel her looking. At more than one thing too. Don't ask me how I know. But I can feel it. She's looking at the empty space. And she's looking at me too. I can feel her eyes moving from one to the other.

But I'm just looking at one thing.

She speaks, spitty now.

'You going to tell me what this is about?'

'It's not an empty space.'

'What?'

I look round at her this time.

'It's not an empty space.'

She glowers at me, stares back over the road, shrugs.

'All right, it's a car park. Only it's got no cars in it. So it's an empty space. Far as I'm concerned.'

'It's where I first lived.'

I got her attention now. She narrows her eyes.

'You lived in a car park?'

'It wasn't a car park then.'

'What was it?'

'A home.'

She leans out into the street to get a better look. I yank her back into the alleyway.

'Don't,' I say.

'There's nobody watching.'

'There's always somebody watching.'

'Let go of me,' she snarls.

I let go. She stays where she is, flicks her eyes over the road, fixes 'em back on me.

'What kind of a home?' she says.

'A shit home.'

I look over the road. And you know what, Bigeyes?

It's weird. Like that other place is still there. Like it'll always be there. Like you could smash away all the houses, clear the rubble out, turn the whole effing street into one great globby piece of nothing, and you know what?

That part of it still won't be an empty space.

Cos ghosts don't leave that easy. And this one's still there. I can feel it.

'They found me outside the door,' I murmur.

Bex is quiet. But I can feel her waiting.

'I was in a box,' I say. 'So they told me later. Might all be lies. Just making up a story. Baby in a box. Kind of romantic, yeah? Long as you're not the bloody baby. But that's what they told me. Said I got left there by whoever my parents were. Or somebody else maybe. Christ knows. But they took me in, the people who worked there, gave me a name.'

'What was it?'

'Never mind. And that's where I first lived.'

'How long for?'

'Four years. Then I got moved on.'

'You *got* moved on?'

'Yeah.'

Bex is quiet again. But I know the question she's going to ask next. And here it comes, clipping into my head.

'What was it like, this home?'

I don't answer. I can't suddenly. I got flashbacks hitting me again. Same ones I always get when I think of this place. Memories without faces, memories without shapes. Not even memories really. Just the feeling of 'em, the fear of 'em.

The pain.

I look at her. I can feel tears pushing up, spite of what I said about not crying. I hold 'em back, just, but I'm struggling and Bex has picked it up. I can tell from the way she's fixing me. She bites her lip, looks away.

A car draws up in the street. We both pull back. I check out. Dronky old motor turning into the car park, ancient gobbo driving. Little kid on the front seat. His grandson, I'm guessing. Same mouth and nose.

They get out, gobbo buys a parking ticket, they trig off down the street. Kid looks about four. Could have been me all those years ago. Same colour hair even.

Bex speaks again.

'What happened to the home?'

I look round at her.

'I burnt it down.'

'Jesus!' she says.

She sticks her head out again to get a better look. I pull her back into the alleyway.

'Stay out of sight.'

'There's nobody,' she says. 'I just told you.'

'Stay back.'

You too, Bigeyes. Cos there's something she hasn't seen, something you haven't seen. A car chunking down from the right. It's not the one those gobbos had down by the school. It's a bigger one.

'Can't see nobody,' says Bex.

'Stay back.'

'Let go my arm.'

Didn't realize I was still holding her. I let go, but I'm watching her cute, like I'm watching the street cute. Can't see the car now. We're too far into the alleyway. But I can feel it.

'Keep back,' I say.

Sound of voices coming close. Nothing to do with the car. Women talking, loud and snappy. We'll see 'em in a moment and they'll see us. Just hope they don't blotch us to the nebs in the car. Cos I'll tell you something, Bigeyes. It's not muffins in that thing.

Don't ask me how I know.

Two dolls, twenties, triked up with lippy, naffing their mouths off. They stop in the opening, see us, fall quiet.

'How you doing?' I call.

'Who the hell are you?' says one.

'Man from the moon,' says the other. 'And his bird.'

Both snigger. But I'm watching the street past their shoulders. Car's stopped. I can see the bonnet. Black motor, engine snorting.

'We got to go,' I say.

'Something we said?' snipes the first woman.

She cackles and her mate joins in. Sound of a car door, another. I grab Bex by the arm.

'Come on.'

'Blade—'

'Come on!'

I pull her down the alleyway, but she's holding back.

17

'Bex, come on!'

The women go on laughing.

'Bex! We got to run! And we can't go back to the street!'

'But this alleyway don't go nowhere. It's a dead end.'

'Just do what I do!'

Sound of hard, gruff voices. Now Bex starts to run. More voices, the women arguing with the gobbos, spluttering, squealing. Sound of a slap, screams, then footsteps thundering after us.

'Come on, Bex!'

We race down the alleyway, round the bend, stop at the far wall. Check behind. No sign of 'em yet. But they'll be here any second.

'What now?' says Bex.

'Over the wall. There's a little courtyard on the other side. Back of a shoe shop.'

'How do you know?'

'Never mind. Just climb over the wall and run like shit.'

'But it's too high!'

'Get on the dustbin!'

She clambers up and over. I'm straight after her,

just in time. Gobbos storm in as I drop down the other side. We hare round the shop and out into the street. Bex turns left. I catch her arm.

'Other way.'

She doesn't argue. We sprint off, both panting. Check over my shoulder. The gobbos'll hit the street any moment. We got to be quick.

'Left here, Bex.'

Past the bank, over the car park, through the bike sheds, down the path, over the fence into the allotment, down to the far end, over the other fence, up to the main road, check behind.

Three gobbos pounding after us. They must have gone the other way to start with, like I hoped they would, so we bought a few seconds. But not many. They're coming on fast.

'What do we do?' says Bex.

I can hear the terror in her voice. I check the road, walk off the kerb, hold out a hand, scream.

'Taxi!'

It pulls over. Bex runs up and joins me. I pull open the door.

'Get in, Bex.'

We pile in the back. I glance at the allotment. Gobbos close to the fence now. If the driver doesn't pull out soon, they'll block the motor and we're done. I look at him. He's turned round and he's fixing us slow, like he's wondering if he made a mistake picking us up.

'Let's go, mate,' I say.

'Where to?' he glums.

'Over the river. I'll tell you where to stop.'

'You got money?'

'Yeah, no problem.'

I feel Bex grab my arm. She's staring at the gobbos sliming close and she's choking up bad. I got to act quick or she'll freeze the driver.

'I got money, mate. It's not a problem. Other side of the river. That's cool.'

He's still not convinced. Bex's hand clamps me hard. I see the grinks spread out. They're walking now, so they don't look suspicious, but they're moving fast and one's cutting into the road to block the taxi. Driver hasn't seen 'em yet. I give him a nod.

'Let's go, mate.' I glance at Bex, give her a peck on the cheek. 'All right, babe?'

She doesn't speak, just clings on. Driver's looking her over. This isn't working. I got to try something else. I lean forward, stare past him.

'Who the hell's that?' I say.

Driver turns, sees the grink in front of the taxi. Gestures at him.

'Move it!'

Grink stays put.

'Get out the way!' shouts the driver.

Grink starts to edge forward. Other gobbos step closer. Hard men, all of 'em. We can't handle this crew. And the driver's not going to help us. But I'm wrong. He twists round, winds down the window, sticks his head out.

'Get out the bloody way!'

Then he ramps up the revs, pulls out and suddenly we're round 'em, tanking down the road. He spits out the window, closes it, glances round. But he's not checking me and Bex. He's checking the grinks. He watches for a moment, then turns back to his driving.

'I've had it up to here today,' he mutters. 'Wanky drivers, wanky passengers, wanky jay-walkers.'

Glances round again. And this time he's looking at me.

'You better have that money on you.'

'I got it.'

'Show me.'

I see the fear back in Bex's face, feel her hand clamp me again. Gobbo's still checking me. He's turned back to his driving but he's watching in the mirror. I reach into my pocket, pull out a note.

Bex's eyes widen, but she doesn't speak.

I hold up the money for the driver to see. He gives a shrug.

'Fair enough.'

'Happy now?'

'Where'd you say you want to go?'

'Over the river.'

'Then what?'

'I'll tell you when we get there.'

He says nothing. But I can feel him still watching us. We got to make this a short ride. The grinks'll have his registration number going round by now. Bex lets go of my arm, leans back. I glance at her.

She's breathing hard, really hard. She's not going

to last, Bigeyes. I'm telling you. She's never going to last. Not in the Beast. She's wiped in her head. Don't ask me what I'm going to do about it. Cos I don't know.

Check out the window.

Yeah, right. See that, Bigeyes? The bastard sights. Some of 'em anyway. There's loads more, if you like that kind of thing. But here's a fistload in one plug. Tourists pay big jippy to see this. Christ knows why. And here's the worst bit coming up.

Mother Grime.

Bitch of a river. Don't give two bells how famous it is, how much history it's got, how many songs and poems and cranky paintings they've done of it. All I know is it's wide and it's deep and it's wet, and I wish we didn't have to cross it.

'Which bridge?' says the driver.

'Next one.'

I catch his eyes in the mirror again. He's not angry like he was, but he's curious. He doesn't know what to make of us. And he's starting to chew over those gobbos. He thought they were nothing to do with us. But now he's wondering.

Bex is wondering too. I can see it in her face. But

she's not wondering about the gobbos. She's trying to work out how come I got money. Well, she'll have to go on wondering, and so can you. Cos I can't talk now. I got to keep fixed on the driver.

He's turned onto the first bridge. Bogeybum I call it. Don't ask me why. I've just always called it that. Yeah, I know. You're confused. Well, I don't care. I told you. I got my own names for the places in the Beast. Get over it.

I got to focus on what I'm doing.

Halfway across. I'm watching cute now, checking cars, faces, and Mother Grime slinking underneath us. God, I hate this river. Don't feel safe, even in a taxi on Bogeybum Bridge. But we're nearly over. And then we got to split.

Fast.

Just a bit further. Wait, wait, wait. Driver's watching me in the mirror again. I take no notice, check round, check again, call out.

'Pull over.'

He pulls over, checks the meter, looks round. I don't

wait for him to speak, just pass him the note.

'Keep the change.'

He raises an eyebrow.

'You serious?'

'Keep it.' I nod to Bex. 'Let's go.'

We climb out. Driver's watching us, frowning. I give him a wave. He goes on watching, then slowly pulls out from the kerb. But he's on his mobile straightaway.

'Come on, Bex.'

'Which way?'

'North side of the river.'

'We just come from there.'

'I want to get back. I don't trust the driver. He's ringing a mate or the police. And the other lot could get hold of him. I got to make 'em all think we're on the south side. Come on.'

She doesn't move, just stands there, trembling.

'Bex, come on.'

It's no good. She's blanked up. I don't blame her. She's blasted over Dig and Jaz, choked up to her head with all that's happening. But I got to shift her and I got to do it quick, cos we're stuck here in full view of every grink who slimes up.

I take her arm, talk soft as I can.

'Bex, listen. We got to get off the road, keep out of sight. Got to do it for Jaz.'

She still doesn't move. Jesus, Bigeyes, I don't know what to do. She's just blobbed there. Got to think of something. I lean forward, give her another kiss on the cheek. She jerks back like I slapped her.

'Stop doing that!'

Pushes my hand off her arm.

'And don't ever call me babe again.'

She fixes me.

'Which way?'

I don't answer, just lead her to the side of the road, down the steps, under the bridge. I don't check to see if she's following. I can feel she is. And anyway, I got to watch elsewhere. Cute as I can.

No sign of danger under the bridge. Couple of duffs curled on the ground. Kids on rollerblades rippling past. Out the other side of the bridge, cut left, cut right, on down the road.

Check behind.

She's still there, scowling at me. I want to help her, Bigeyes. I know you don't believe me but I do. I feel responsible. I am responsible. She's right to be angry. If it weren't for me, the grinks wouldn't have taken Jaz.

Wouldn't have murdered Dig.

Or Trixi. They were looking for me in the bungalow, remember.

So it's my fault. Like so many other things. I don't blame Bex for hating me. I hate myself too. But I got to get past this. Got to make my hatred do some good. Got to save it for the grinks. Or there's no point fighting back.

Won't change Bex's feelings about me. Whatever I do, she's going to rage. But I can't let myself care about it too much. Got to focus on what I can do, not what I can't. Funny though, what she said about me kissing her.

I mean, think about it, Bigeyes. Couldn't she see I was acting the first time? And just trying to help her the second? Christ's sake, like I'm ever going to want to kiss her, even on the cheek.

She speaks suddenly. 'Blade.'

Different voice. Still angry but something else too. Sadness, despair, can't tell. I look round. She's stopped, middle of the pavement, and she's crying. I walk back to her. Don't know what to do. She goes on whacking out tears.

'Bex, we can't stop here.'

She looks me in the face, stares hard for a moment, then pushes past and heads on up the road. But she's walking blind. I can tell. She's just . . . tramping on. Not watching, not seeing, not caring. I catch her up, take her arm.

'Bex, not that way.'

She stops.

'It's where you was heading,' she mutters.

'We got to cut down here.'

I point to the right. She glances that way, sniffs.

'Another alleyway.'

'Yeah.'

'So that's it, is it?' She wipes her eyes with her sleeve. 'Where we're going to be living from now on. Alleyways.'

'We got to stay out of sight.'

'Yeah, yeah.'

'We can't take the big streets, Bex. There's too many people watching. Even the alleyways are dangerous. Cos they know we'll be using 'em.'

'Not much point then, is there?' She glares
me. 'Might as well give up on Jaz now. Cos you
going to do nothing. You know where she is. But a
you're going to do is creep round alleyways. Till they
catch us.'

'Bex—'

She turns away, plods down the alleyway. I check
round, check again, follow. She's trigging slow, shoulders hunched. I feel so bad now, Bigeyes. I got a plan,
got an idea what I can do, but it's so risky, so hard to
crack, and harder still with Bex in tow. Specially when
she's like this.

She stops suddenly, turns.

'You're shit, Blade. If I knew where Jaz was, I'd go
straight there.'

'Yeah, you would.' I fix her. 'Cos you're stupid
enough to think that would work.'

She slaps me hard in the face. I wince, but don't
move. Didn't see it coming, but I see the next one.
Other hand, whipping in. I let her hit me, and again,
and again. She's still crying, great sobby tears, and
she's lashing out big time, hard, heavy slaps, like she
wants to split my face.

I stand there, take it, then suddenly she stops, half-falls over me, chin on my shoulder, arms loose.

'You bastard,' she mutters. 'I hate you so much.'

'I know you do.'

She doesn't answer, just stays there, flopped against me.

'Bex, listen . . .'

She starts to whimper. She's still got her arms hanging loose, her chin dug into my shoulder. I hesitate, put an arm round her, wait for her to pull back, spit, slap, whatever. She doesn't do anything, just stays like she is.

I check round us. Got to keep doing that, Bigeyes, whatever's going on with Bex. Nobody in the alleyway. Flick a glance back at the street. Nebs passing by, all muffins so far. But we can't stay here long. Got to wig it off the south side before the grinks snap in.

'Bex . . .'

She shrugs my arm off her, pulls back. I try and fix her. She won't let me, just stares down at the ground.

'Bex, I'm in it for Jaz, OK?'

She doesn't answer.

'I'm in it for Jaz,' I say. 'Like you. But I can't just walk in there.'

She lifts her eyes, glimmy with tears.

'They wants you,' she mumbles. 'Them guys. I don't know who they is. And I don't know what you done, cos you ain't saying nothing. But I know they wants you. And they don't want Jaz. So it's easy.'

'It's not.'

'It is.'

She leans closer.

'You give yourself up. And Jaz goes free.'

She pauses.

'And before you ask—no, I don't care what they do to you.'

I shove past her, stomp down the alleyway. She calls after me.

'But you ain't going to help her, are you? Cos like I say, you're shit!'

I stop, clench my fists. OK, that's it. She wants to bomb words? So do I. I turn, drill the troll—then catch a movement behind her. Higher than the street, higher than the roofs of the houses. Up on the bridge where the taxi dropped us off.

Two gobbos checking round.

Might not be grinks.

But I got a bad feeling about 'em.

'Bex, we got to go.'

'Yeah, yeah,' she whines, 'we got to go. We always got to go. Find another alleyway, find another excuse.'

From up on the bridge comes a shout.

'There!'

One of the gobbos is pointing at us. Bex turns, sees him, looks at me. And the terror's back in her face.

'Come on!' I yell.

She doesn't argue this time. She's sprinting down the alleyway so fast I can't keep up with her. I let her race ahead. Doesn't matter, long as I can see her. She's running blind, like she was walking blind a moment ago, not seeing, not thinking.

But I'm doing both.

Checking the dark corners, the places to watch, and thinking, even as I run. Alleyway cuts into a side street just ahead, and then we got choices. Not many and they're all bad, but we got a chance.

Can't run our way out of this. There'll be grinks crowding the area in minutes. And we'll never hike another taxi cos they don't come down these streets much. So it's hook a smelly or hit the snakehole.

Both crappy options.

Plenty of smellies rumbling about. Number 49 goes over the next bridge and there's a stop round the corner. Trouble is—what's the chance of one turning up just when we need it? Not much. We'll run past the stop but it's a long shot.

Which case we'll have to smack it with the snake-hole.

But that's even more dangerous. They'll have dronks watching all the stations. Got no choice though. It's get away or get caught. And we might just slip through if we play it cute.

'Bex!'

She's still tearing ahead.

'Bex! Cut left at the end. But check it's clear first.'

She doesn't check, just cuts left and disappears from view. Crazy troll. She's got no idea. She's got to think what she's doing, even though she's scared. She could be running straight into 'em. I'm praying they're not waiting for her round the bend.

We'll soon find out.

End of the alleyway, stop, check behind.

No sign of the gobbos from the bridge. Check into the street. No grinks in sight, just a couple of workmen digging up the road, and Bex pelting on. Bloody hell, Bigeyes, I got to haul her back somehow.

Trouble is, I don't want to shout. Draws attention. But wait a sec. She's stopping by herself. Turns, stares back at me. She looks like a hunted deer. I run down to her, hoping she won't bundle off again.

She doesn't, just stands there, gasping. I catch the workmen looking, flick 'em a smile, make like it's no bum gripe. They don't smile back. And they don't look away either. I ease Bex off to the left.

'Where we going?' she moans.

'Bus stop.'

'Bus stop?'

'Yeah.'

But it's like I told you, Bigeyes. Not a smelly in sight.

'OK, Bex, this way.'

I pull her into the next street.

'Now where we going?' she mutters.

'Just follow, OK? Cut the shit. We're surrounded and we've only got minutes to do this.'

'Do what?'

'Catch the tube.'

She stares at me.

'You got money for it?'

'Yeah.'

'How come? You didn't hardly have no money when we ran away. So you said. And then you pulls out a note for the taxi driver and—'

'Shut it, can you?'

I'm checking round as we walk, checking cute.

'I haven't got time for this, OK? We got to shift. Just do what I say. I'll tell you about the money later.'

She shuts up, thank Christ.

We walk on, fast. I want to run but it's a bad idea now. Too obvious, specially if there's eyes round the tube station. Least the day's getting busy. I'm hoping there'll be a good crowd hitting the snakehole. If there is, we might just snick in among 'em.

Right at the end of the street, down to the bottom, check round. Next bridge getting closer, nebs swarming round it. Hard to tell who's a muffin and who's a grink. And that's not all. We got porkers to think about too. Don't forget them.

No sign of any yet but they won't be far.

Cut right, away from the bridge. Keep to the side of the road. Cars sniffing past. Check out the carriageway. Might just be lucky with a taxi, but I doubt it. They don't usually like this road cos it's hard to pull over with the bus lane.

Here's the tube station. Left, down the lane behind the sandwich bar, out the other side, check over the road. Good—lots of nebs triggering down the steps into the snakehole. Nice muffiny-looking nebs too. One or two dronks hanging out either side of the entrance but they look more like duffs than grinks.

Walk on, slow, stop behind the refuse van.

Bex bumps into me from behind. I round on her.

'Watch what you're doing.'

'You stopped sudden,' she grumbles.

I fix her, wait for her to fix me back.

'This is serious, Bex.'

'I know.'

'Then do what I say.'

I wait. Her eyes have wandered off again. They look so scared. I can't find the heart to bollock her like I should.

'Bex?'

'What?'

'Do exactly what I say, OK?'

She shrugs.

'OK.'

'You don't walk with me. You don't talk to me. You don't look at me. You check me out now and again. But casual, yeah? Not so anyone can see you do it. We mustn't look like we're together. Can you do all that?'

'I'm not an idiot.'

'It's important, Bex. OK? Keep apart from me all the time. I'll get the tickets. Just follow me, get on the same train, sit apart.'

I reach into my pocket, pull out some coins.

'There'll be a newspaper stand on the platform.'

'How do you know?'

'Never mind. Buy a magazine. When you're sitting down, pretend you're reading it. Cover your face as much as you can. Only don't make like you're trying to do it. You know what I mean?'

'I just told you. I'm not an idiot.'

'And don't catch anyone's eye. Or look up at any cameras.'

'Can we just go?'

I check round again. It all looks plum. That's what bothers me. I walk up to the kerb, stop. Feel Bex move up behind me. Jesus Christ, she's forgotten what I said already. I don't look round, just mutter over my shoulder.

'Stay back. You're too close.'

Feel her start to edge away. I mutter again.

'No, don't move back now. You'll make it too obvious. Just let me get ahead, then follow. Keep some distance between us. Like I say, I'll get both tickets. I'll leave yours where you can pick it up. So watch close so you don't miss it. Let's go.'

Can't wait any longer, Bigeyes. It's now or never.

But there's already four new gobbos hanging round the entrance to the station. They might not be trouble and we still got to try. But I'm less confident than I was ten seconds ago.

And I wasn't confident then.

Over the road, slopey walk, eyes down. Bex hasn't followed. I can feel that without looking. She's hanging back like I told her to. Least she's got that bit right.

Just hope she starts walking soon. She's leaving it a bit long.

Check back.

Here she comes. Slow walk, like me. Turn back to the entrance. Time to brisk up. If there's grinks here, they'll block us straight off. They won't let us hit the steps. But we might just have got here first.

Two gobbos to the right. Don't like the look of 'em. They don't stop me but they're checking behind me, maybe watching Bex. I chuck her another glance. Still crossing the road after me. Doesn't catch my eye.

Good girl.

Keep doing that.

Into the entrance, and no one's stopped me. Over to the ticket machine, money in, snap the tickets, over to the barrier, check behind. She's a little way back, further than I want her to be, but there's no one between us. Just hope she claps this.

I drop to my knee, fiddle with a shoelace, leave one ticket on the ground, straighten up, walk through the barrier, on towards the escalator. Check behind, and there's Bex through the barrier, coming on too.

Down the escalator, through the tunnel, onto the platform. Check the sign. Train coming in two minutes. Bex appears, takes no notice of me, walks past, buys a newspaper from the stand, waits further down the platform.

Two gobbos trig up, the ones I saw earlier. They walk on, stop between me and Bex. She flicks open the newspaper, buries her face in it. She's bummed this one, Bigeyes. Should have bought a magazine like I told her to. She doesn't look right holding a news-paper, specially that one.

If she'd got a tabloid, it wouldn't be so bad. But she's bought a heavyweight bloody broadsheet. Who's going to believe she reads that thing for fun? I know why she got it. Cos it's big. Cos it covers her face. But she didn't think. Jesus! She couldn't stand out more if she tried.

Both gobbos are looking at her.

But here comes the train.

She hears it, shakes down the newspaper, folds it up, checks my way. Train pulls in, stops, doors open, nebs pile off. I wait for the gobbos to move. They don't, just stand there, talking. I feel Bex watching me again.

I walk up to the door, wait for the gobbos again. They move up to the next door, stop. I step on the train. They do the same. Bex climbs on. Same door as the two guys. Walks to the end of the carriage, sits down, flicks open the newspaper again.

Gobbos walk over to her, stand nearby. I walk down the other end, find a spot, sit down. Doors close, train rattles off. Check round. Carriage half full. Muffins, no question, apart from the two gobbos.

Can't make up my mind about 'em. Got to play this cute, got to watch without watching, fix their shadows and get ready to cop their spit if they make a move on Bex. Don't think she's even noticed 'em. She's got the newspaper over her face again.

Train clatters on, pulls into the next station.

I get up, walk down the carriage to the middle doors. The gobbos are still at the end, close to Bex. I can see her watching me over the top of the newspaper. I take no notice of her, stand by the door, wait for the train to stop.

It slows down, judders, comes to a halt.

Bex stands up, folds up the newspaper, edges past the gobbos.

Doors open.

I get off, walk down the platform past Bex's door, feel her slip behind me. Check over my shoulder. Gobbos are climbing off too. I walk on, waiting, watching.

Jump back on the train, next carriage.

Bex does the same.

Doors close. Train moves off. No sign of the gobbos but there's panic in Bex's face. It's freezing her up, all this. She starts to walk over. I turn away. Mustn't let her talk to me. She's got to stay cool or we're goosed. The gobbos aren't in this carriage but that means nothing. They could easily have got back on the train.

And if they did, we'll know they're trouble.

I don't sit down. Plenty of spaces but I walk past 'em all to the end of the carriage. Turn round. Bloody Christ! Bex is still walking towards me. I turn my head, sharp as I can. But I can still feel her coming on.

What's wrong with this troll? She's got to pick up signals. Even if she's freaked, she's got to pick up signals and act her part. I turn my back to her and hold on, swinging with the train. She steps alongside me.

'Go away,' I mutter.

'I'm scared, Blade.'

Her voice is so small. Makes me think of Jaz. I glance at her. She's gone right inside herself. Eyes blank, like she's folding up. I mustn't let her do this. Those gobbos could well be on the train. And even if they aren't, there's still grinks all around us.

I take my eyes off her. Got to play my part, whatever she's feeling. Got to act like we're not together. But I can feel her trembling now. She's leaning against me and she's shaking. I murmur to her.

'It's all right, Bex.'

'I'm so . . . I'm so . . .'

'It's all right. I won't let anyone hurt you.'

I feel her body press against mine. She's still shaking. Train pulls into the next station.

'Are we getting off?' she breathes.

'Don't know yet.'

I check the carriage, edge towards the door. Feel Bex take my hand, squeeze it. I don't look at her. It's no good. I got to check things super-cute here. Only I can't let go of her hand. I should do. I know I should. Cos this is madness. But I can't make myself. For her sake. Didn't think I'd ever say that.

She squeezes my hand again.

'It's all right, Bex. It's all right.'

Doors open.

I lean out, check the station. No sign of the two guys. But there's three other gobbos on the platform. Just standing there, watching the faces of the nebs getting off. I don't trust 'em. Whip my head back inside the train.

'We're staying on, Bex.'

She says nothing, just goes on holding my hand. Nebs piling into the carriage now. I look round at Bex, give her hand a squeeze, then slip mine free. Lean close, whisper.

'Go and sit down there. Have another read of the newspaper.'

She's not going to do it, Bigeyes. Look at her face. She's so choked up she'll never move. But I'm wrong. She glances at me, same empty eyes, then walks down the carriage, sits where I told her, opens the newspaper.

I'm tense as a spring now. Check up and down the carriage. It's almost full. Only one space left, opposite Bex. Might as well take it. Better than standing here. Can't be seen so easy.

I walk over, check round, sit down. Just hope Bex
keeps her head and doesn't talk or anything. Glance at
her. She's got the newspaper open and she's holding it
so high I can't see her face. But I can see another face.
On the front page. A photo.

Of me.

Age eleven.

And a headline.

WHO IS BLADE?

Don't suppose Bex has seen it. She'd be reading the
article otherwise. I lean forward, couple of inches.
Hard to see clear but I can scrape most of the words.

It's like I suspected. Porkers have rounded up the
gang. Xen probably cracked her mouth. I'm guessing
conscience hit her. Or the trolls did. Someone needed
to. Anyway, they're in custody. Tammy, Sash, Xen, Kat.

No mention of Riff. What a surprise. He's probably
dribbled under a stone, hoping the trolls'll lick the
swill for him. Makes no difference. The talking's
started, the name Blade's out there, plus my old police
photo, and it's a big, big story.

First the body count. Trixi and Dig. The gobbo in the hospital, the dunny in the snug. Paddy, Lenny, and the grunt. No details about the grinks. Probably cos the porkers can't work out who they are.

Then the other stuff.

Bex and Jaz still missing. Gob from the gang about what happened at the old prof's house. Witness report from 'an elderly Irish woman who befriended the boy'. Bless her sweet, beautiful heart.

Then the speculation. Who is Blade?

And you know what, Bigeyes? That's how it's always been. Who is Blade? Cos here's the thing. No one knows. Some nebs think they do but they're wrong. I'd had a hundred names by the time I was ten and Blade was just another.

You want to know who Blade is?

I'll tell you.

I'm whoever you want me to be.

I'm a story you make up for yourself.

To the trolls, I'm a kid who pissed on their turf. To the other nebs in the old city, the few I let near me, I'm whatever name I gave 'em. And it wasn't Blade. So to them I don't exist.

Different in the Beast. Cos the name came from here. From Becky originally. But by the time I ran away, it was all anyone called me. Porkers, grinks, gangs. They all knew the name. And they all thought they knew me.

But I'll say it again.

I'm whoever you want me to be.

The newspaper says I'm a fourteen-year-old boy who's been in trouble with the police all his life. A kid who's been missing for the last three years, who's dangerous with a knife. A kid who might have killed.

Now read the last sentence of the article. Go on. Read what it says.

Who is Blade?

You see? They still don't know.

But I'm not the only story on the front page.

MARKETS IN TURMOIL AS GLOBAL CRISIS DEEPENS.

Yeah, right. Is that supposed to be news? Well, it's not to me. I could have told you years ago this was going to happen. Business hitting the grime. Economies round the world getting blasted. Don't believe me? Well, I don't care. I knew it was coming.

Cos I know some of the bastards behind it. Trust me, it's not just greedy bankers grubbing the patch. They're part of it, yeah, but there's more to it than just them. The real slime's somewhere else, somewhere nobody's looking.

The storm's breaking, Bigeyes.

So you better get ready.

Train rumbles on through the snakehole.

Bex lowers the newspaper, catches my eye, looks away. I stand up, edge towards the door, feel her do the same behind me. Train shivers into the next station, slows down, stops. Doors open.

I check out. Looks clear.

Onto the platform, Bex just behind. She's left the paper on the train. Into the tunnel, up the escalator, through the barrier, up the steps towards the street. Bex starts to catch me up.

I stop, nod her back.

She stays where she is. I walk on, slow. Got to check the exit, make sure it's cute. Lots of nebs busying about, but I can't see any danger. Doesn't mean much. The biggest danger's always the one you never see.

Glance round. Bex is still standing where she was. I turn, slip out into the street, cut right, check behind. She's following, keeping back like before. Long as she stays like that, we're plum.

Trouble is, she probably won't.

And even if she does, I got to keep checking her.

So you might as well know, Bigeyes. I've made my mind up about something. It means using someone from the past, someone I've been trying to keep out of this, and it'll be a tough gripe. I'm not happy about it at all.

But I got to try.

Cos to put it bluntly, I can't drag Bex much further.

First up, she's dronky at doing this. Ducking, dodging, kissing shadows. She'll shunt us both if we carry on like this. And second, she'll never slam what I got to do tomorrow. No way. She'll hate it so much she'll try and stop me.

Maybe you will too.

Cos I'm telling you, Bigeyes, you won't like it either.

But it's something I got to do, OK? It's for the best. Only Bex won't see that. Like I say, she'll try and stop me. And I can't have her crabbing my gut. Or you. So remember that, Bigeyes. I'm giving you fair warning.

Keep your distance when tomorrow comes. You'll know when I'm squeezing the flame. Cos you'll hate what you're seeing. But get in my way and you're dust. Anyway, that's for later. First things first.

Round the corner, hugging the wall. Keep close to the offices. Twisty little street. Nebs everywhere, jacking the pubs and sandwich bars. We better get some food ourselves. Haven't eaten for hours and I can't believe Bex hasn't guffed about it yet.

But we got to hit another place first. If it hasn't closed down in the three years I've been away from the Beast. Jesus, it's still there. See it? The old charity shop. Crappy as ever.

Check it out, Bigeyes. Would you want to buy from a place like that? Even for charity? Just as well I only want two things. Stop outside, check round. Bex is hovering a short way back.

I nod her towards the doorway on her right. She slinks into it, but sticks her head out and fixes me.

'Wait in there,' I mouth.

She disappears.

No problem in the shop. Two minutes and I'm out again. Down the street to the doorway and there's Bex, looking scared. She stiffens at the sight of me and I got a feeling she's been crying again. But she speaks.

'What you got in that bag?'

'Two big coats. With hoods. What colour do you want?'

'Neither.'

'Take one.'

'I like what I got.'

'Take one. Pull it over what you got. Should be big enough.'

'What for?'

Jesus, Bigeyes. I can't believe she just asked me that.

'We got to keep changing our appearance, Bex. Come on. Choose one.'

She checks in the bag.

'Shit colours,' she says.

'They're meant to be. I want 'em boring. So they don't stand out.'

She sniffs.

'I'll have the brown one.'

I check round, make sure no one's watching, pass
her the coat. She puts it on, frowning.

'You paid for this?'

'Yeah.'

'What with?'

I don't answer, just pull the grey coat out the bag,
rip off my old coat.

'Ain't you keeping that?' says Bex.

'No.'

I turn my back to her, swap the jippy from my old
pockets to the new ones. But she sees.

'You bastard,' she mutters. 'You got great frigging
wodges of money. Where'd you get all that?'

'Tell you later.'

'Tell me now.'

'I'll tell you later. We got to go. Come on.'

She grabs me by the arm, snarls at me.

'Tell me now!'

'It's not safe to talk here.' I lean close. 'I'll tell you
later. I promise. But not here.'

She doesn't answer. Just glares. I lower my voice.

'Do what you did before, OK? Keep me in sight but
stay back. And watch for signals.'

She looks down, trembling. She's on the edge, Bigeyes, over the edge maybe. I can't be dealing with this. Not here. It's too dangerous. I got to move and I got to make her move with me.

I check the street, slip out, cut down the pavement, glance behind.

She's following, but she's walking like a dimp. She's got to smack this. There's a speed, a right speed, and she's got to sting it. Not too fast, not too slow. Sometimes you got to run, sometimes you got to creep. But sometimes you got to just take it cool and cute.

She's moving too slow. Shoulders hunched, eyes like stones. Glances over, skims my face. This is bad, Bigeyes. She's like a dead troll looking for a new grave. I got to get her off the street.

I stuff the bag and my old coat into a bin, trig back, check round, take her hand.

'Come on, Bex.'

I walk her on faster. She doesn't pull back, try to let go. Lets me lead her. But her hand's limp in mine. No pressure, nothing. Maybe it's best. She still looks dead to anyone watching but at least she's moving and I can cut off the street just down from here.

By the post office, see? Little side road. Takes us somewhere I can give her a break. Before we crack the next bit. Long as we get to the post office before some neb asks her what's wrong.

On, on.

Almost there. Just a bit further.

Shit, two porkers coming from the left, gobbos.

Bex hasn't clapped 'em. But she's not clapping anything right now. She's got her head down, and she's crying again. Jesus, we're clemmed if they're coming for us.

Bex looks up, catches my eye. She still hasn't seen 'em. I'm watching cute. Checking her, checking them. They might not be hitting us. Hard to tell. But they're heading over. I lean close to Bex, speak soft.

'When I let go your hand, walk on and cut down that side road. By the post office. Got it? Don't look at me. And don't look left. There's two policemen coming over.'

I feel her head start to turn that way. Squeeze her hand tight.

'Don't. Keep looking straight in front.'

Her head stops, turns back.

'Good girl.' I hang on a moment longer. 'OK, I'm letting go now. Just do what I say. Cut down that road and keep walking. There's a little Methodist chapel halfway down. Wait for me in the doorway.'

I let go her hand, cut across the street. Porkers coming on. One's talking into his spinny. Other's checking round. Flicks a glance at me as I slip past. But I don't feel him stop, or his mate.

Up the pavement, into the sandwich bar, over to the counter, check through the window. Porkers have stopped on the other side of the street. A third porker's joined 'em, a woman.

Bex has disappeared.

'You ordering or just standing there?' grumbles a voice.

Look back over the counter. Chubby-face gobbo watching me, snappy eyes. Over the street I catch the porkers moving. Heading towards the post office. Sound of a snort. Glance back and see Chubby frosting his brow. I cut in before he does.

'One tuna and mayo, one ham and salad, one cheese and tomato, one egg and cress.'

'Hungry, are you?'

I don't answer. I'm checking the street again. Porkers have disappeared. Can't tell from here if they've scuffed the way Bex has gone. Or should have gone. Cos I wouldn't bet a bean on her going where I told her.

They've all wigged it anyway. Got to shift my stump case there's trouble. Bex can't handle anything right now. If she ever could. Glance back at Chubby.

He's taking his time, dicking the bread, packing the slices, wrapping everything neat with his fat fingers. Nice job but I wish he'd chug up. I got to blast on quick. Check the street again. And now there's new grime.

Two more gobbos, and they're not porkers.

Or muffins.

Don't ask me how I know.

It's kind of a smell. They don't look different from the other suits shaking shadows up and down the street. Smooth, confident, clickety-clean. But they are different. I'm telling you.

'Something to drink with that?' says Chubby.

'Two bottles of mineral water.'

I catch a look. I'm still watching the gobbos but I catch it. Glance back.

'Please,' I say.

He smugs up, like he's just made a point, fetches the bottles, stuffs everything in a bag. I hand him a note, check the street again. One of the gobbos has pulled out a mobile. Other gobbo's checking round.

'There you go,' says Chubby.

He's holding out the bag.

'And your change,' he adds.

I take everything, step towards the door, stop. Two more gobbos have turned up. And I know one of 'em. I've seen him before. He's from the old days. Can't remember his name. But he's one bastard dronk.

Question is: how to get over to Bex without 'em seeing me.

More nebs crowding into the sandwich bar. Street's getting busier. That should help a bit, but I still need these gobbos to move, even if they don't blast out. Right now they're just blobbing there, checking round. I can't shift till they do.

Chubby chimes in again.

'You all right?'

He's halfway through serving some woman but he's peering across.

'Got a problem?' he calls.

Yeah, yeah. He wants me off his stack. I got to move or he'll make something out of this and the gobbos'll clap it. Out of the sandwich bar, down the pavement, checking the other side. The grinks are wandering down towards the post office, all four. They stop, just by the side road down to the Methodist chapel.

I slip behind a parked van, watch cute.

Two of 'em talking into mobiles. Other two flicking round. This is bad, Bigeyes. Bex hasn't got a chance if they cut down that side road. She'll be slumped in the doorway of the chapel and they'll walk right up to her.

Hang on.

They're not heading down the side road. Cos there's the porkers coming up it. Don't know what this means. They haven't got Bex with 'em. And they're not interested in the four grinks. They're walking past 'em.

And now the grinks are splitting.

Edge round to the end of the van, watch 'em go. They're not sticking together but trigging off down different streets. Porkers stop just down from the post office. Then they split too.

Over the street, stop at the post office, check round.

Crowds still crunching about, but no porkers, no grinks. None I can see anyway. Down the side road, checking doorways. Methodist chapel's further down but she could have stopped anywhere. It's Bex, remember. She doesn't think cute, even when she's not choked in the head.

Nothing in the doorways. Couple of alleyways, little narrow ones, dead ends. She's not in there. On down the side road. Getting a gripey feeling, Bigeyes. I know we haven't hit the chapel yet but I can't throw it off. She's not going to be there. Don't ask me how I know.

What did I tell you? Empty doorway.

Check round. No sign of her. Could have wigged it at the sight of the porkers. Should have done, if she was thinking good. But her head's blown. She could be anywhere. Check round again.

Iron fence either side of the chapel. Poky little cemetery round the back. I slapped a night in there once, huddled against a gravestone. Middle of winter, rough as death. I was nine years old.

Bex won't be in there.

Only way to the cemetery's through the building or over the fence. And she wouldn't have the blitz to climb this thing. Too high, too visible, pointy spikes at the top. She'd never go for the fence if she saw the porkers coming. They'd spot her too easy. She'd blast off down the road.

But I got this feeling, Bigeyes.

So I better cop a glint in case.

Check left, right. Clear for the moment but it won't be for long. There's too many nebs buzzing. Lob the food bag over, up the fence. Got to do this quick, but it's a bastard to climb. How did I get over this when I was nine? Spikes at the top nicking my trousers. Yank 'em free. Down the other side.

Land soft, pick up the bag.

Concrete here but there's grass round the back. Only a tiny cemetery but it's hidden from the road.

Good choice if Bex was trying to hide. But she won't be here. She can't be. Don't know why I'm even checking.

End of the building, stop, glance back. Nobody in the road, nobody fixing me from any of the windows opposite. No sounds inside the chapel. Pretty sure it's all locked up. Round the back of the building, into the cemetery.

And there she is, slumped against a gravestone. Same one I used all those years ago. She's crying her head off. I run over, kneel down.

'Bex.'

She doesn't answer.

'Bex, you did good.'

She goes on crying. I lean closer.

'You did real good. Coming here. It's a great place to hide.'

She looks at me, teary eyes.

'But it didn't work, did it?'

She slumps her head again.

'Cos you found me.'

I sit down next to her, lean back against the

gravestone. Don't know what to say. She slammed me with that one. Wasn't expecting it. Wasn't expecting to care either. What's going on, Bigeyes?

This caring.

And Bex, of all people.

Caring about Jaz, caring about Mary. That makes sense.

But caring about Bex? And what she just said?

She's crying again, head down, like she's forgotten I'm here. I want to do something, make her stop. Can't think of any words that'll do it. And I'm not touching her. She'll bite my hand off. I know it.

I pull out the sandwiches and mineral water.

'I got something to eat, Bex.'

Doesn't even look at it.

'Tuna and mayo.' I hold it out. 'Or we got ham and salad, cheese and tomato, egg and cress.'

She takes no notice. I put the tuna and mayo in her lap. She doesn't touch it, but she doesn't flip it off either. Crying's getting softer. More of a moan now. Head's still slumped on her chest, like she doesn't want to see anything.

See me anyway.

Check round. Big high walls round this part of the cemetery. We're not visible from any angle. She chose good. Probably an accident. But we're cute for the moment. Cold but cute. She stirs suddenly, wipes her eyes with her sleeve, fixes me, looks away again. Takes the sandwich, stares at it.

'Go on, Bex. You got to eat.'

'Piss off.'

She takes a bite, couple more, then flings the sandwich away. It plunks another gravestone, drops on the grass, spills out the tuna. She slumps her head again, but she's not crying now. Except inside. I can feel it. And it hurts. Hurts me, I mean.

Don't know why.

I look down. Can't face her suddenly. She's so full of pain.

And that's when they start.

The flashbacks.

Can't work out why they're hitting now. And yet . . . maybe I do. I'm looking at Bex again and remembering something she said that time she was rowing me ashore from the motor cruiser. About what her father did to her.

Don't suppose she's thinking about that now. She's in a different kind of pain and it's tied up with Jaz and Dig, and me. But pain's pain and she's unlocked some of mine. I hesitate.

'Do you ever . . . ?'

I stop, look down again. Flashbacks stabbing hard now. Bex is quiet but I'm tensing bad. Got to stop this, got to calm down, front up.

'Ever what?' says Bex.

I take a breath, force out the words.

'Do you ever get memories you can't see, but . . . you still know what happened?'

I look at her now. She's watching me. No expression.

'That home,' I say. 'Where I lived up to the age of four.'

'The one you burnt down.'

'Yeah.'

I bite my lip.

'Those four years . . . they're like a cloud. I can't see anything. Not even the faces. But . . . I know what they did to me.'

I look away. A seagull's flopped down by the tuna

sandwich. Nabs at it, flies off. I follow it, arcing over the rooftops. Bex speaks.

'Can't you see none of it?'

'Just the very last bit. Setting fire to the place. I remember that. And getting caught. And bustled off.'

'Where to?'

'Another home.'

'What kind?'

'Tougher.'

'To turn you into a good boy?'

'Yeah.' I stare after the seagull. 'Only it didn't work.'

'You ran away.'

'Lots of times.'

'And they kept catching you.'

'Yeah.'

Seagull's gone. Just rooftops left. And flashbacks. Clear ones now. I reach down, take one of the sandwiches. Hold it out to Bex. She takes it without a word, starts eating.

I pull out another one, take a bite. Egg and cress. Can't hardly taste it. I try and eat but it's no good. Drop the sandwich on the ground.

BLADE

'I was dead by the time I was four.'

'Eh?' says Bex.

'Dead in my heart. Got moved from place to place. New rules, new punishments. Supposed to make me better. Just made me more angry. Started playing with knives. Found I was good with 'em. By the time I was seven, I was dangerous.'

'So they called you Blade.'

'That was later. When I was ten. Friend of mine started calling me Blade. I was showing off to her. Tricks with a knife. Nothing bad. She wasn't the kind of person you do bad things to.'

'She?'

'Yeah. She.'

I go quiet. I'm not ready to talk about sweet Becky. Specially to her namesake.

Bex doesn't push it. I go on.

'They had other names for me when I was seven. Loads of 'em. I was in trouble everywhere. You name it, I was up for it. Out of control. I was ripe for the picking. So they picked me.'

Silence.

Bex takes a slow breath. I glance at her.

'They catch 'em young, pre-teen. And they know what they're looking for. Kids they can train. Kids who are damaged and want to be part of something. They're the easiest meat. The kids clinging to gangs. The ones who think respect comes from defending your postcode.'

I watch the pictures moving in my head.

'And then there's the others. The kids who don't want to cling to gangs. The loners. The ones who are so badly hurt they don't give a shit. They just want to lash out, hurt back. They're the pick of the lot. Train 'em good and you got a weapon like nothing on earth.'

Bex takes another slow breath.

'That's you,' she says. 'Ain't it?'

I don't answer.

'Ain't it?' she mutters. 'You're a weapon.'

I nod.

'If I was dangerous when I was seven, I was lethal a year later.'

'How lethal?'

'Get caught inside my throwing range and you're dead. If I want you to be. There's nothing I couldn't hit.

And hand-to-hand, where it gets creamy——I was even better at that.'

'Really proud of yourself, aren't you?'

'No.'

'You sound like you is.'

She pauses.

'You've killed.'

'Is that a question?'

'Maybe.'

'Well, I don't want to answer it.'

'Think you just did.' Bex frowns. 'So who are these people? The ones what train little kids.'

'Part of a criminal network.'

'What's it do?'

'Same things other criminal networks do. Drugs, trafficking, prostitution, money laundering, protection, usual shit. At the bottom end.'

'The bottom end?'

'Yeah.'

'Meaning what?'

'Meaning that's all I'm telling you right now.'

She studies me, gives a slow scowl.

'So has it got a name? This . . . network?'

I shake my head.

'It's got to have a name,' says Bex.

'Only a handful of people know it exists.'

'But you said it's a network. So there's got to be loads of people in it.'

'There are. Thousands. All over the world. They just don't know they're in it.'

'What?'

'They don't know they're in it. Cos they're being used by the people at the top. And there's only a few of them.'

Bex is watching me cute.

And I know what she's thinking.

She's thinking, if there's only a few nebs at the top who know what's going on, how come I do too? And you're thinking the same thing, aren't you, Bigeyes? Well, think away. Cos it's none of your business how I know.

'You're lying,' says Bex. 'There's no way you could keep a network like that secret. Specially from the people in it. They got to know. Some of 'em anyway. And it's going to leak out. It'll be on the internet somewhere.'

'Well, next time you hit a search engine, type in "criminal organizations" or "secret societies" or whatever. You'll get all the ones everybody's heard of. But you won't find this one. Cos like I say, there's only a few people who know it's there. And they're not telling.'

She runs her eyes over me.

'But you know it's there. So how come you're not telling?'

'Cos it won't make any difference.'

'What do you mean?'

'It won't be enough to bring the bastards down.'

And you know why, Bigeyes? Cos they're too clever. Too well protected. I'm talking about the slime-heads at the top. The spikes further down are more vulnerable and the grinks at the bottom are ten a penny.

But even they're hard to nail.

Cos no one knows who they are. Half the time, they're brought in from abroad. Come in, do a job, get paid, hike out. Ask no questions. No one to ask anyway. Only neb you deal with is your pay-daddy. All you know is what he tells you. And all he knows is what his pay-daddy tells him.

Lenny and the grunt could have come from anywhere. Probably abroad. Paddy too. And the scumbo in
the hospital. As for the wackies we already got here—
the pushers, pimps, beefheads, and bruisers—they get
used too. Why not cream the home-grown shit when
it's sitting on your doorstep?

And it all works the same way.

You only ever see the dreg above you, never the
one above him.

Gangs too, they get used, and they're the easiest
to shunt. The teens who think they've stepped up, hit
the scene, started shifting the big grime. They're not
smart enough to see they're just the playthings of
other people.

But I shouldn't crow.

Cos that's what happened to me.

Though in a different way.

Another silence. Bex finishes her sandwich. I hand
her the last one. She takes it without a word, starts
eating. I hold out a bottle of mineral water. She takes
that too, sips a bit, looks at me. I guess her question
straight off.

'They wanted me cos I was useful,' I say.

She shakes her head.

'They wanted you cos you could kill.'

She frowns.

'You ain't never going to do nothing for Jaz.'

'I want her back as much as you do.'

'Then where is she?'

'I don't know.'

Bex gives a snort.

'That guy in the house said you know where to come.'

'I know where they want me to come. But that's not the place where Jaz is. She could be anywhere.'

'Then we ain't going to get her on our own, are we?' Bex stares at me. 'Might as well call the police.'

'They won't find her either,' I say. 'Not alive anyway.'

Bex turns her head away sharp, like I slapped her. I lean forward.

'But that doesn't mean we can't get her back.'

Darkness. Took its time coming. Can't believe I

got Bex to wait here this long. She's slept a bit, spite of the cold. Snored even. Funny, grumpy kind of snore.

'Bex.'

She stirs.

'Time to go,' I say.

She yawns, fixes me with her eyes. She's still angry with me. More than that. She still hates me. Don't think she believed a word of what I told her earlier. Maybe you didn't either, Bigeyes.

Well, that's your problem. And hers.

I got enough worries of my own right now. I'm dreading the next thing we got to do. I'm telling you, it's buzzing my brain. First cos of Bex. Got no idea how she's going to react to what I got planned. And second cos of the person we're going to see.

Best-case scenario: we scrape through.

Worst-case scenario: don't even think about it.

Bex is still watching me. There's so much in her eyes now. Anger and hatred—I already told you about them—but there's other stuff too. Sadness, fear, mistrust.

Disappointment.

Yeah, disappointment. In me. I can see it. Like she'd let herself hope for a moment that I might just be able to do something. But she's woken up and the hope's gone. Cos her belief's gone. And now the eyes are spitting at me.

Jaz is dead, they say, and it's your fault.

'We got to go, Bex.'

Stand up, walk to the side of the building. Glance round at Bex. She hasn't even asked where we're going. Doesn't care. Look at her face. See? Doesn't give a shit any more.

'Bex, listen . . .'

'What?'

'You got to have some money.'

I pull out the wodge, hand it to her. She takes it, stares, counts the notes.

'Jesus!' she mutters. 'Five hundred quid?'

'Take it.'

She looks up at me.

'Going to tell me now, are you? Where you got it?'

'Riff's pockets.'

'What?'

'Back at the old house. Remember? When we ran downstairs and out? I went through Riff's pockets first. Thought he might have left his jacket cos he had to leg it so quick.'

'I didn't see you.'

'I know you didn't.'

She checks me over.

'Got lucky, didn't you?'

'Yeah.'

I'm not telling her about the twelve grand I got in my other pockets. Didn't think Riff would still have it on him. But it was worth checking. And like Bex said, I got lucky.

'How much you got left?' she mutters.

'About the same as you.'

She doesn't believe me. I can tell from her face.

'Come on,' I say. 'We got to find a taxi.'

'A taxi?'

'Yeah.'

'Didn't go too well last time we got one.'

'Should be better now it's dark. But listen. We got to act normal. Like we're together.'

'I ain't bloody snuggling up or nothing.'

'I don't mean that. Just act like we're mates.' I pause. 'Try and forget you hate me.'

'Yeah?'

She leans close, eyes hard.

'And you reckon that's possible?'

I don't answer. She clenches her teeth, grits out the words.

'You killed Jaz. You know that? You killed her. And Dig. And Trixi. They all died cos of you. And Christ knows how many other people there are.' She wipes the spittle from her mouth. 'And you really think it's possible I could ever stop hating you?'

She turns towards the street.

'Let's go.'

'Bex—'

'And don't bother telling me where we're heading. Cos I don't care.'

This is bad, Bigeyes. Worse than I feared. She'll sink us both in this mood. There's that many grinks out watching. I run round in front of her.

She stops, glares.

'Bex, I know you're angry with me—'

'You're frigging right I am.'

'But we still got—'

'Yeah, yeah,' she sneers. 'We still got to be careful. Yeah, yeah.'

'It's dangerous, Bex.'

'Like I give a shit.'

She brushes past me. I run ahead, get between her and the fence.

'Bex.'

She stops again.

'Bex, do you want to just split?'

She stares back at me, raging, hating.

'Do you want to just split?' I say.

She doesn't answer. Just stands there, breathing hard. I stare back at her, wait. She watches me in silence, then looks away.

'Let's just go,' she mumbles.

I cut to the fence, check up and down the road. Looks cute but I can't see too far from where we are. Got to take a risk. I glance back at Bex.

'I'll go over first. Wait till I give a nod, then climb over. Follow me but stay back, like we're not together.'

'You just said we got to act like we're together.'

'In the taxi, I meant. When we're walking, you stay

back. And keep your eyes open.'

Check again. Looks clear.

Over the fence, down the other side. Glance up and down the road. Nod to Bex. She climbs over, quicker than I thought she would. Down the pavement, keeping close to the buildings. Check back.

She's following, about the right distance but she's too close to the road. I nod her towards the shadows. Walk on, cut left, left again, stop.

Got to watch ourselves. We're close to Panky Station and there's always lots of nebs round there. Grinks'll be checking it too so we can't use the taxi rank. We'll cut over the road and hook a cab on the other side.

Check round. Bex is still keeping back, but she'll have to move in again soon. I bung her a look. Doesn't catch it. I try again. This time she nods back. I got to stop her doing that. But not now. She's trigging over.

I wait till she's close, then cross the road. She follows, just a bit apart. Traffic building up. Taxis and smellies mostly. Hit the other side, whip a glance at Bex. She joins me, checks the road.

'There's one,' she says.

I got my hand out already. Taxi pulls over, window slots down. I lean through, give the driver the address. He pulls a face but doesn't say no. I climb in after Bex. She's acting good so far. Not friendly but cute enough. Catch the gobbo's face in the mirror.

He's not happy. And I don't blame him.

Who wants to drive into the Den?

But he sets off. Heading for Mother Grime. I lean forward.

'What you going this way for, mate?'

'Who's driving, me or you?'

'Just wondering.'

'There's road works,' he grumbles. 'So we got to cut down to the river and round.'

'Fair enough.'

I lean back, move closer to Bex. She doesn't pull away. I look at her. She's staring out the window and I can tell she doesn't want to talk. That's cool cos I don't either. Long as she doesn't fizz up again or do something stupid.

Cos she could. Any moment. Check her out.

She's still boiling inside.

I look away, out the window. Feels weird seeing the Beast again. Like nothing's changed in the last three years. Hard to think some nebs like this place. I'll always hate it.

'Sorry about this,' says the driver suddenly.

I check ahead. Couple of cars pranged together and a porker directing the traffic. Driver sniffs.

'Shouldn't be a problem. We'll get round this way.'

He cuts off right. Good choice. I'd have done the same. End of the road, left again and there's Dingdong and the old Toffhouse straight ahead, and Mother Grime flowing past 'em. Left at the bottom and now we're moving fast, river on the right.

I glance at Bex. She's staring out the window at the prickly water. I can't bear to see it, even in the dark. We're shifting now, like the driver wants to get this over with. But I can understand that.

The Den's the Den.

It's not the only bad district—there's plenty more in the Beast—but you wouldn't want to live there. He'll drop us off and wig it. And he won't be looking for a fare back. Cos you don't hang about in that place.

Can't believe this guy. He's hammering the motor. Going to get stopped if he clatters on like this. Check right. Mother Grime still loping past. Spinner bright and clear on the other bank. And there's the Coffin straight ahead.

History's shithole.

Jesus, I hate monuments.

But now it's behind us and we're cutting on east. River's fallen back. Good bloody riddance. But I can't think of that. I got my head full again. I got pictures flooding like before, only now it's all the same one. The face of a woman. Last time I saw her, she said she'd kill me if I come back.

Maybe she will.

Taxi's still cranking too fast. Or maybe it's me. Shit, Bigeyes, it is me. I'm looking at the speedo and it's cute. Driver's spot on the limit. It just felt like he was belting. It's not him moving too fast. It's me. My thoughts.

My fears.

Cos I'm scared that what's coming is coming too quick.

On, on. No monuments here, just dark dives, dark

streets. Shadows on corners, shadows in windows, shadows in shadows.

'Left at the end, mate,' I call.

'I know where it is,' comes the answer.

I catch a glance from Bex. Still angry, still bubbling underneath. Looks away again, like she doesn't want to see me. Driver cuts left, jets through the estate. Knows his way round. I'll give him that. Even in the Den.

End of the estate, right towards the shops, left by the old cinema. Pulls over, fixes me. I take no notice. I'm sniping the streets.

Group on the far corner. Five of 'em, teenagers. Three dronks, two trolls. Another group over by the playground. Six dronks. No, seven. No sign of any gobbos.

Driver gives a cough.

I hand him the money, snap the change. We climb out. Taxi screams off. Figures moving either side of the street. Not towards us. Just moving.

As they watch.

Bex edges close.

'I don't like this,' she murmurs.

'It's OK.'

I turn left, away from the figures. They don't follow. Got to walk a bit. Didn't give the driver the real
address. I gave him the next street. Just in case. Check
back. Still not being followed, just watched. Right at
the junction, down the road.

And there's the house.

Same as it always was. Crumbly, tatty, tiles loose.
Upstairs window boarded. Cheap curtains downstairs.
I can see a shape moving against 'em, a shape I know.
They flick apart, close again. And I know she's seen us.

I'm trembling, Bigeyes. And I can't stop myself.

The shape moves again inside the house. I take a
breath, walk up to the door, Bex beside me. I don't
bother to ring. Sound of footsteps inside, then a pause.
A long one.

Door opens, and there she is.

Scowling.

'Hello, Ruby,' I say.

She looks old, Bigeyes, ancient. Can't believe how bad
she looks. Can't be more than thirty. Used to be a

stinger, spite of working the streets. Smartest black woman out there, the alleybums used to say. Know what they called her?

Black Magic.

Well, check her out now. Is that what three years does to you? Or maybe just the last three years. Cos they won't have been good for her.

She's dressed bad too. Never used to be. Didn't look scrubby ever. Class act, whatever she was doing. Too good for the clapheads who spiked her over. Looks wasted now. Dronky skirt, dronky blouse, half-on, half-off.

But the eyes watching me are the same as ever.

Jesus, Bigeyes. It's hard to know who hates me more.

Ruby or Bex.

'This is Becky,' I say.

Ruby sniffs.

'No, it ain't.'

Same voice. Rich and husky. She flicks an eye at Bex.

'That ain't Becky.'

Turns suddenly, leaving the front door open, sets

off up the stairs. I catch a glance from Bex. Step in, up the stairs after Ruby. Hear Bex close the door behind and follow.

Rickety landing. No carpet. Two floorboards missing. Bathroom and bedroom, nothing else, both doors open. Smell of vomit from one, candles from the other.

Ruby's in the bedroom, back to us, facing the boarded window. Walk in, Bex on my shoulder, stop, check round. Chaos of clothes, blankets, empty crisp packets. Single bed, no sheets. Ruby looks round, steps aside.

And something closes round my heart.

Cos there she is.

My little beauty.

My black-skin, fairy-eyed beauty.

'That's Becky,' Ruby says.

The photograph stares back, straight at the camera, straight at me. Like the last time I saw her, three years ago. Could have been taken that day. Both of us just eleven. I find I can't breathe. All this time I've just had memories. And now it's like she's here. I know she's not. It's just a photo on top of a dresser, candles burning either side of her. A little shrine to a memory.

But it feels like she's here. And I want to hold onto that.

Ruby squares up to me.

'That's Becky,' she snarls.

I feel Bex stiffen. Ruby's eye flickers over her, falls on me again.

'Bad idea you come back.'

She pauses, flame-shadows ripping her cheek.

'I don't got nothing no more. No food, no drugs, no drink. Spend all my shit on candles.' She pauses again, watching me. 'But I do got this.'

Opens a drawer, pulls out a gun, points it at me.

'You got sixty seconds to tell me what happened.'

'Jesus!' shouts Bex.

'You can go, girl,' says Ruby. 'It's him and me.'

Fixes me hard.

'And you got fifty seconds now.'

Bex scampers out the room, down the stairs. No sound of the front door but I hear her pacing up and down. I stare back at Ruby.

'I'll talk. But we got to deal first.'

'You're not here to deal! I told you last time—'

'Yeah, you told me you'd kill me.' I take a step

closer. 'So why'd I just walk up to your front door?'

'Forty seconds.'

'Must be thirty by now.'

'Piss off!'

She grips the gun with both hands. I take another step closer.

'I'll tell you about Becky. If you look after my friend.'

The pacing stops below. Sound of footsteps creeping back up the stairs. Ruby's arm wavers, straightens again. Her eyes are hard. But her mouth's trembling.

'Is Becky alive or dead?' she says.

'Help my friend and I'll tell you.'

Footsteps on the landing. They stop outside the room. I can hear Bex breathing as she listens. Ruby sways on her feet. Looks bombed, choked. Could easily shoot me by accident.

'Help my friend,' I say. 'And I'll tell you about Becky.'

Ruby lowers the gun, slumps on the bed. Stares over it.

'We used to sleep in this thing,' she mutters. 'Becky and me. Only bed we got. So we crammed in together. Not much room but we managed. Like we always done. Till you shoved your stinking face in.'

Glares up at the door.

'Who the hell are you?'

Bex is standing there, watching.

'I'm Becky,' she says. 'Honest. It's my name. But some people call me Bex. Blade always does. Don't know why he called me Becky just now.'

Ruby gives a snort.

'Then you ain't worked out what a manipulative little bastard he is.'

'Yeah, I have,' says Bex.

They stare at each other, neither speaking.

Hiss of candles, then silence. Just my heart pounding as I look at the photo again. Sweet Becky. The shadow of a dream. And you know what, Bigeyes? There's something of Jaz in that face.

No question.

Yeah, I know. You're thinking it's just me wanting to see it. And you'd have a point. I mean . . . there shouldn't be anything. Black girl age eleven, white girl age three. But there's something I noticed before. Something I spotted that very first time I saw Jaz's face, when she was hiding under the bed.

She reminded me of a snowdrop.

And that's it. The thing they both got. Cos even though Becky could never look like a snowdrop, she always looked like a little flower. To me anyway. Same as Jaz. Another little flower.

Jesus, Bigeyes.

I hope they're not both dead.

'Is Becky alive?' says Ruby.

I look at her. Mouth's still trembling. Eyes still hard. But she's forcing 'em like that. They're hard cos she's angry. But they're also hard cos she's holding tears down. Taking all her will to do it. Taking all my will to do this too.

Be hard back.

But I got to be hard. Got to force myself. Cos I got to deal.

Or Ruby'll never do what I want.

'I'll tell you,' I answer, 'if you promise to look after Bex.'

But Bex has got her own ideas.

She moves so quick I don't have time to stop her. Jumps over, grabs my hair, shoves me back against the wall, face thrusting close. I catch Ruby staring from behind, confused, scared. Bex doesn't see her. She's fuming too hard at me.

'Tell her,' she breathes. 'Tell her what she wants to know.'

'Keep out of it, Bex.'

'Tell her!'

She whips round, blasts a question at Ruby.

'Kid in the photo, she your daughter?'

'Yeah.'

'And you don't know what's happened to her?'

'No.' Ruby looks down. 'But he does.'

Bex whirls back, eyes flashing. I try to squeeze from her but she crabs me against the wall, hands round my neck.

'Is Becky alive or dead?'

'Bex—'

'Tell her!'

'Bex, listen—'

She lashes out, a full-on punch. Claps me on the cheekbone, smacks my head into the wall. Another punch. I try and block it, miss. Plunges into my chin. And here's her hands tight round my throat, squeezing.

But here's Ruby, too, and she's not after blood.

'Easy, girl, easy. He's not worth it.'

Bex clings on, eyes digging into me. Then suddenly she lets go, turns away, claps a hand to her face. Ruby puts an arm round her shoulder, looks over at me.

'You better go.'

'Ruby—'

'I look after your girl.' Ruby frowns. 'You don't got to do nothing for me. Just go.'

I reach into my pocket, pull out the money I had ready. Ruby glances at it.

'Don't want no money.'

'Five hundred quid.'

'Don't want no money. Not from you.'

'I'll leave it downstairs on my way out.'

Bex has started crying, her face buried in Ruby's shoulder. But she looks up, glowers at me.

'You was always going to dump me.'

I don't answer.

'Like you dumped Jaz,' she goes on. 'Like you dump everybody. Becky too, yeah?'

I shake my head.

'Bex, listen . . . I wanted you to stay with Ruby cos those people . . . the ones after me . . . they never knew I came to this house. Becky was a secret friend. I kept it quiet from everybody. So you should be safe here. And Ruby's got a kind heart. Even though she hates me.'

I feel my words fall like stones. Ruby and Bex just stand there, silent, bonded against me. I look at the photo. Becky's still smiling. Like nothing's wrong. Like nothing ever was.

'Bex?' I say.

She doesn't speak. I look round, fix her.

'I'm going for Jaz, OK? Cos I think she could still be alive. But I got to do it on my own. You can't help me. You'll just get in the way. So you got to stay here with Ruby. And wait till I get in touch.'

Bex watches me for a moment, then lifts her face, spits. The gob catches my neck, dribbles down. I wipe it off with my sleeve, look at the photo again. Turn to Ruby.

'Becky's dead,' I murmur.

No answer. I bite my lip.

'I'm sorry.'

I wait for her to ask me more. What happened, where the body is, who did it. But she doesn't. She just stares back at me. No tears, no trembling, no shouting. Just a long, unwinking gaze. Then a slow darkening of the eyes, like a shroud's being pulled over 'em.

I turn away, cut down the stairs, stop at the bottom. Drop the money on the mat.

Slip out the door.

Hood up, down the street, moving fast. Shadows on both pavements, front and behind. Might not be interested in me. Can't tell yet. But I got to be careful with all this jippy on me. And worse still.

The chance of being recognized. There's plenty of nebs'll know me in the Den, even if they haven't seen me for three years. And plenty more who'll know about me from the news.

Wound in my head doesn't help. The newspaper article mentioned the knife slash so that's going round too. I've stopped wearing the bandage and my hair hides the mess pretty good, but the cut's still visible.

Bit angry with myself for not sorting it better. I should have fixed something to cover it up.

Still, the Den's a big place and I'm hoping I'm cute round here. I was dead careful when I used to see Becky. Didn't want to plug any grime on her and Ruby, so I kept away from their house as much as possible. Never even went in there before today.

Let's hope none of these nebs have worked out who I am.

'Blade,' mutters a voice.

Shit.

It's coming from over the road.

'That's him,' says the voice.

Not talking to me direct, just gobbing to a mate. But it makes no difference. They've hooked me first go. Flick a glance over. Two dronks, about sixteen, tracking me down the other pavement. Couple of trolls saun-tering behind 'em.

Just watching so far. Don't know if they saw me come out of Ruby's place. Jesus, I hope not. This is bad, Bigeyes. Didn't think I'd get skewed in this street. Even with my name banging the news.

Don't recognize any faces.

More figures ahead, lounging by the bus stop. Same sort of age. Glance behind. Shadows following, both pavements. Think it's all teens whipping this street. Three or four talking on mobiles. Keep catching the same word.

'Blade.'

'Blade.'

'Blade.'

It's like a whispery echo. They're not firing it off, just talking low to each other. Hanging back too, so far. I'm sensing they're wary. They know what I can do, or they've heard about it from others, and the gump on the news has linked me with murders, so they're staying safe for the moment.

I got to use this.

Walk on, steady pace. Leave the hood up. They've smacked who I am but I'm keeping my face dark. Gang still lounging by the bus stop ahead. Four dronks, two trolls, all watching. Over to the right, a couple snogging on a bench. They break apart as I draw close, stare at me.

I check the six standing.

They've stiffened, two of the guys fingering their

pockets. Both the trolls too. Guy from the bench stands up, his girl still clinging to him. He shakes her off, fixes me. Big dronk, quick eyes, beanie on his head.

'Blade,' he growls.

Not so wary, this crew. Least three of 'em looking to rip. Which case I got a problem. Cos I can't fight 'em, not without a knife. So it's a straight choice. Run or spin their heads. Yeah, right.

We both know I'm a crap runner.

So it's a bum flush. I got to sting one on 'em. If I can.

Fix the big guy. No question he's the beef. Crack him and I crack the others. He's walked out in front of 'em but he's stopped now. I keep walking, walking, walking—stop.

Arm's length from him.

Right hand in my pocket.

I don't move. Not a muscle. Just stare out from under my hood, head back in the folds. He's watching me close, trying to see more of me. This is where it gets skinned, Bigeyes. Next few seconds. I nail him or I don't.

He's looking for someone he can beat in front of his girl. Someone he can smug about, someone with a reputation. He's heard about me and he's thinking—

this kid's small. It should be a whack stuffing him over. But he's peering hard just to check I'm not the one thing he's scared of.

A psycho.

And that's what I got to make him see when he looks inside my hood.

It's not about fighting now. It's about will and chill. Dead eyes, dead heart, and letting him see both. I stare up at him, cold, cold, through his face and out the other side.

He's not moving now. He was edging closer, but he's stopped. He's as still as I am. Now's the moment, Bigeyes. If he moves back, I got him. If he stays, I'm hanging.

He stays.

I watch, wait, breathe out the words.

'There's blood all down your body.'

He doesn't speak, doesn't move. I lean close, whisper.

'Cos I just cut your throat.'

I hold his eyes, keep my right hand in my pocket. Reach up with my left, smooth back my hood so he sees the wound. Ease the beanie off his head. Slip it on mine.

Wait.

He stares back, face like stone. I stay still, watching his eyes. Doesn't matter about the rest of him. He's clenching and unclenching his fists—I can feel it—and his body's rippling with tension, but it's all in the face now. He blinks suddenly, takes a step back.

I go on watching. He won't move quick. He's got to save some spit with his crew, and I got to let him. They'll jump me if I play this wrong. But they're splitting already. Big guy's turned and he's stomping over to the other pavement.

Rest of his slugs follow, checking me as they go. None of 'em speaking but they're watching wary. Didn't hear what I said to their dronk cos I talked so low. But they've picked up who won.

So he's still got a problem.

Trouble is—so have I. Cos there's more shadows closing in. Only here's something else. A smelly. Number 24. Oh, you beauty. Doesn't cruise the way I want to go but who gives two bells? It'll get me out of here.

Pulls over at the stop, doors open.

Nobody gets off. I check round. No dregs belting in but they're all watching. Climb on, pay the driver, sit down, front seat, back to the other passengers, hood up again, over the beanie. Doors close. Bus grunts off down the street.

I keep my eyes in front. Don't need to check behind. I clapped the other passengers when I got on. All muffins. Driver's no gripe either. Hardly looked at me. Probably guffed to his brain picking up teenage slugs. The Den's crackling with 'em so I guess another one makes no difference to him.

I'm thinking hard. I've paid for five stops but I might get off sooner and change buses. Point is, Bigeyes, I know where I got to go, but I got lots of nebs to avoid. Maybe smellies are the best way to get about this time of the evening. Long as I keep my head down and watch cute.

Street's behind us now and we're turning right. Past the park, past the old school, through the shopping centre. None of this has changed, Bigeyes. It's like I just left yesterday. Almost expect to see Becky standing outside the Half Moon Café.

Over there on the left. Got it?

Dronky pit but we used to meet there after she finished school. I never went. To school, I mean. Not ever.

But Becky did. Used to like it, she said. She had this little satchel and she'd wait for me outside the Half Moon, and we'd go in and have milk shakes and sticky buns, and she'd pull out all her exercise books, and show me what she was doing.

I wasn't that interested. I just loved being with her, listening to her talk, hearing her laugh. She had this kind of gurgle. She'd find something funny and start chuckling, and then she couldn't stop. It used to make her whole face light up. I loved being with her.

But then Ruby found out she was meeting me on the way home from school. Becky hadn't told her. And Ruby said she had to stop, cos I was bad shit. Which was true. So I thought up other ways me and Becky could meet. Secret ways Ruby didn't know about.

And that's when everything went wrong.

But I can't think about that now. Cos I got a new problem. Smelly's pulling over at the next stop, there's two gobbos waiting to get on, and I recognize 'em.

Grinks.

Seen 'em before, both gobbos. I know which spike

they work for. And what they can do. Tell you something else, Bigeyes. They're not here for a ride.

Grinks drive. They crack about in cars. They don't
jump on tube trains or buses. Only time they hit the
snakehole or hook a smelly is when they're looking for
someone.

I got to get off. And I got to time it right. Won't be
easy cos I'm the gig.

The reason they're here.

So they'll be watching cute.

Out of the seat, hood still up, beanie low. Slip
down the bus to the middle door. Faces flip up at me
as I pass. No problem with 'em so far. Couple of old
dunnies. Boy with his mum and dad. Gobbo listening
on headphones.

No one's taking much notice.

Check round. Moment the grinks get on, I got to
get off. Won't work if they've seen me from the road.
Or if they already know I'm on the smelly. They won't
get on at all. One'll be waiting by the middle door,
other at the front.

Bus stops.

Doors open.

I duck my head, keep as low as I can. Glance round. Nobody's waiting outside the middle door. But no one's got on at the front either. Driver calls out suddenly.

'You getting on or what?'

I flick a glance at him. He's shouting into the street. Sound of a mutter, both gobbos. They're not answering the driver. They're mumbling to each other. I see the driver turn.

Catch his eye. He's getting angry. First he's got two gobbos hanging about in the street, now he's got the kid with a beanie blobbed by the middle door. And no one's moving. In a moment he's going to bawl back at me. Ask me if I'm getting off or staying.

And the grinks'll pick up I'm here.

Then I see it. The first of the grinks getting on.

Just the top of the guy's head.

I duck further, edge out the middle door, foot on the street. Check round the side of the bus. Shit, the second grink's still standing outside. Hasn't even started to get on. I need him to follow his mate or I'm plugged.

He sniffs, flicks his head, a little backward tilt. I've

seen him do that before, Bigeyes. It's a mannerism. Makes him feel important, like he's sneering down on everybody.

Don't ask me how I know.

Hasn't looked my way yet. But he could any moment.

Come on, you bastard. Get on the smelly.

Shadow appears, top right corner of my eye. First grink's moving towards the middle of the bus. Couple more seconds and he'll see me standing here, one foot on, one foot off.

But I still can't move till Flickyhead gets on. Shadow moves closer. I got to go, got to risk it. Even if the other grink stays put. Off the smelly, down towards the back, low as I can. I'm waiting for the shout, the thump of footsteps.

Nothing.

Just the sound of the doors closing, the bus pulling away.

Creep to the side of the road, slip behind a parked car, check round. Smelly's rumbling off down the street. Can't see either grink. Wait, check round. Got to make sure they didn't both get off. But there's no sign of 'em.

BLADE

Straighten up, breathe hard. I'm knotted up, Bigeyes.

And I'm still stuck in the Den.

Right, change of plan. Forget about using smellies. Dimpy idea. The grinks are obviously checking everything. Can't use the snakehole either. Taxi maybe, if I see one and it looks safe. But I don't suppose there'll be many in the Den right now. Nobody goes snacking for a fare in this trough, specially after dark.

OK, I know what I got to do. And we better shift, Bigeyes, cos time's ticking. So stay close and keep your spark fresh. We got to see everything.

Over to the other pavement, down the path, left at the church, over the square, past the bank. Check round, all the time. Plenty of nebs to keep an eye on. Muffins so far, even the teens in doorways, but we got to watch.

Every second.

I'm keeping the hood up and the beanie pulled low. That dronk turned out to be useful. Beanie hides the wound and it's warm too. Least I don't stand out too bad here. Lots of other kids punching the streets and most of 'em look like me in the darkness.

But I still got to be careful. Got recognized down Ruby's way, so anything can happen.

Shadow moves down to the left. Might not be anything. Walk on, steady pace. Shadow shuffles, falls still. It's a duff, sitting there. Shaven-head guy. Can't be more than eighteen. Stares up at me, face like a grave.

Maybe that'll be me one day.

Eh, Bigeyes? Four more years and I'll look like him.

If I live that long.

Closer, closer. He's still watching me. I wait for him to call out. He's going to ask for some jippy. And I can't give him any. Not cos I don't want to. I just can't stop. It's too risky.

But he doesn't call out. Just watches. I walk past, on, on. Stop, turn, go back. Flick him a coin. It falls in his lap. He looks down at it, back at me, says nothing. I walk on. End of the street, left, down to the bottom, and there it is, over the road.

The Prince William.

Got to be the ugliest pub in the Den. And that's saying something, Bigeyes. But I'll tell you what. It's got one big advantage. Lots of nebs use it and most of 'em aren't too brained up.

Check it out.

Lights on, clunky music, sound of laughter. Check the traffic. Smelly rolls past, motor bike, another smelly. Empty road. Except for something sticking over the edge of the kerb.

Something round.

Walk over.

It's an old football. Pick it up, squeeze it. Lost a bit of air. Dronky thing. Some kid probably flipped it on purpose. Check round. Cars moving down from the top end, couple more the other way. Turn my face, let 'em pass, turn back.

Give the ball a bounce, catch it.

Trig over the street.

Prince Willy's getting noisy. Some gobbo's started up a song. Round the back, into the car park. Lots of motors there already. Bounce the ball again. Hold it still. Slip into the shadows, crouch.

Wait.

Won't stay quiet for long. Not Prince Willy. Here we go.

Car pulling in.

Slip off my coat, push it out of sight. Not the place for a hood. I got to look like some kid who's just nipped out of his house. But I'll keep the beanie on. Grip the football, watch. Cute motor, stops, other end of the car park.

Four dolls.

They get out, laughing, head towards the pub.

No good. Let 'em go. Never mind why, Bigeyes. I know what I'm looking for and they're not it. More cars, two of 'em. No, three. Now it's looking promising.

Young gobbos. Three in the first car, four in the second, two in the third. They spill out, slam the doors. One of 'em sees the dolls hitting the pub porch, calls out.

'Hey, girls! No rush!'

Other gobbos leer and strut. Dolls take no notice, disappear inside the pub. All the gobbos out now, cocking their stumps round the car park. Easy piss, Bigeyes. You got no idea what a whack this is. I've checked 'em all out. Any one'll do.

I step out, bounce the ball, bounce it again.

'Hey, kid!'

One of 'em's sticking me with his eyes.

I bounce the ball again. They all fix me. And now it's playtime. They're bollocking their heads off, shouting for the ball.

'On me head, boy!'

'Here, mate!'

'C'mon! C'mon!'

I walk in among 'em. Chuck the ball up. They're like flies on jam. Couldn't be easier. They don't give me back the ball, but that's cute. I don't want it. They kick it, head it, lose interest, hack it off into the road, slack over to the pub, hooting.

I wait till they've disappeared, pull out the car keys. Couldn't make up my mind which motor I want. So I creamed two lots of keys. One from the gobbo with the best car. Other from the guy who pissed me off most.

No contest really.

Got to leave the flash one. I'd love to poke it about but it's too risky. Every neb on the street's going to turn and cop a glint at that one. I'll take the other motor. More of a dingo so it's safer. And like I say, the guy pissed me off. Sniggered at me as he booted the ball away.

Back to the side of the car park, pick up the coat, put it on. Over to the flash car, check the pub again. All clear. Leave the keys on the bonnet. Some other dronk might want a free ride. No, hang on. Guy wasn't that big a dungpot. He can keep his motor.

Stick the keys on the front wheel.

Over to the dingo. Unlock it, get in, eyeshine over the tricky. All cute. Key in the ignition, turn. Engine fires. Check the petrol gauge. Off we go.

Out of the car park, left down the road, up to the top, left at the lights, on to the roundabout. Christ, Bigeyes, feels so weird driving round this patch again. I used to jack motors round here for the hell of it.

Past the playing fields, down to the railway station. First time I saw Becky was outside here. She was with a mate but she smiled at me. I'll never forget it. Didn't say anything. Just smiled. Same smile like she had in the photo.

But that first one was special. Whipped me up big time. Made me feel so happy I had to buzz round the corner and smash a window. That old warehouse, see it? Window's round the back. They probably still haven't fixed it.

That's what Becky did to me. Just by smiling. Made me feel like I was worth something. And it was even better when she talked to me. First person to do that. Proper talking, I mean. That's why I loved her. First person to talk to me. First person to care.

Maybe the last one too.

Only . . . no.

She's not the last. I know that. Cos things have changed. I never would have expected it. But Mary cares about me too. Don't ask me why. I was spitty with her in the beginning. Didn't trust her at all. But I do now. And I know she cares.

If she's still alive.

Got to stop thinking like this. It's blamming my brain. And I got to slow down too. I'm driving too fast and you know why? It's cos I'm shook up over Becky and Mary. And now I got Jaz in my head. Like she's ever anywhere else.

And she's shaking me up too.

Slow down, dimp. Slow bloody down.

Got to drive legal, Bigeyes. There's that many nebs

looking for me now. Porkers to the right, see? Too late. You missed 'em. Look better next time. There were two of 'em, women.

Left, down to the bottom, onto the main road. We're heading west, case you're wondering, but we won't be for long. Just a bit further towards the centre, then we cut right and slam the north-east.

Cos there's a place I got to go.

Before I sort out the big stuff.

Got a busy night ahead of us, Bigeyes. And before it all starts, there's something else I got to do. Off the main road, down to the right, round the parade of shops. There used to be a takeaway here. Little kebab shop. Smelly place but quiet.

There it is.

Only now it's pizzas.

Who cares? Pull over, glance round. Feels cute but I got to watch good. There's no part of the Beast that's not dangerous. Check pockets, shift some of the jippy. Stuff a few notes round my dingers.

Out of the car, into the takeaway.

Back again, safety belt, lock the doors. Bolt down the pizza, sink the Coke. Start up, back to the main

road, up onto the flyover. Right, Bigeyes, look ahead.
Go on, straight ahead.

Check him out.

The Beast.

One big bastard, isn't he? Even in the darkness
you can't miss the size of him. Check out all those
lights. And you know what? You're only seeing a tiny
bit of him. Like his little toe. He's a giant, Bigeyes, an
effing giant.

And he's got more ways to kill than you could ever
know.

Yeah, yeah. You're thinking here he goes again.
Banging on about the Beast. You're thinking, for
Christ's sake, it's just another big capital city. Got its
scum, got its dark side, like any other capital city, but
most of the nebs are OK.

And maybe you're right. Maybe most of the nebs
are OK.

Trouble is, I've never met 'em.

I've only ever met the others.

Down the other side of the flyover, on towards the
centre. Least we've left the Den behind. That's a good
feeling. Just wish it was going to last. Cos now we're

turning right and heading for the Grinder.

That's what I call it anyway.

Different kind of area. Not so beaten up as the Den. Bit more jippy in some of the streets and not so many gangs. But there's bad shit there, mostly spinning drugs, and plenty of hard dronks who'll know who I am.

So I'm not stopping long.

It's blast in, blast out.

Past the brewery, past the school, past the start of the motorway, over the roundabout, right at the lights. Feels good to be heading away from the centre. But I'm doing it again, Bigeyes. Driving too fast.

Slow down, slow down.

Porkers heading the other way. They flash past. Check the mirror. They've gone but now there's another police car, and it's coming up behind. Squeeze the wheel. Check the mirror again.

They might not suspect anything. Might just be driving this way. But I was belting it a moment ago. No question, I was way over the speed limit. Jesus, Bigeyes, if I get plugged cos of something so stupid, something I did myself, I'll never . . .

They're pulling out.

Eyes in front. Keep the speed steady. I can feel 'em, Bigeyes. They're drawing level. Don't look at 'em. Keep driving, keep driving, nice and legal. They're hovering now, just sitting there, edge of my blind spot. I can feel 'em checking me.

Maybe the gobbo who owns the car has reported it missing and the porkers are on it already. Or maybe they're just thinking this kid looks too young to have a driving licence.

They're edging past. This is the moment. If they flash me to the side of the road, I'll pull in and wig it over the barrier. I might just get away. But they're not stopping. Thank Christ. They're driving on.

I slow down, breathe hard, let 'em disappear ahead.

Take the next exit.

And we're in the Grinder.

Told you it was different, Bigeyes. Check out the houses. Smarter, see? Better cars too. Like I say, more jippy round here than in the Den. But remember the other thing I told you. There's hard nebs here too.

Trust me.

So keep watching.

Cut right, round the edge of the estate. Good news is we don't have to go too far into the Grinder. I chose a cute spot when I cooked this one. You probably think you know what's going to happen next, right?

So I'll tell you something straight up, Bigeyes.

You're wrong.

Don't look at me like that. I can read your chirpy little brain. It's going, 'I remember the bridge over the stream. I remember the overflow graveyard. He's got some diamonds stashed away. Or some money. Or both.'

Well, stuff your brain. Cos it's wrong.

Half-wrong anyway.

Let's get this over with.

Other side of the estate, right at the junction, down the lane, on towards the railway line. Over the bridge, slow down, check round, pull over. Lights off, cut the engine.

Darkness.

Heart's pounding, eyes skudding about. Calm down, calm down. Wait, wait, wait. Open the door, ease out, listen. Close the door, listen again. Yeah, Bigeyes, take it in.

Sounds and silence. Both together.

The sounds of cars rumbling round the Grinder, the traffic further off. The sounds of the Beast. The deep heavy breaths as he rolls and roars.

And then the silence.

The silence of where I am, standing here by the railway line. Like I'm in a little glass bulb. My silence. Just my thoughts whispering inside me.

Check round.

No shadows moving. None I can see anyway. Think the railway line's deserted. Hope so anyway. You sometimes get duffs slapping it round here. They find a spot among the bushes either side of the railway fence. Don't ask me why.

Dronky place to sleep. Must get woken every time a train rattles by.

Still, I think we're on our own for the moment.

Come on.

Over the fence, down to the tracks, listen again.

No tinkling in the rails, but we got to be careful, Bigeyes. I nearly got slammed here once. Never heard a thing in the rails and suddenly there's a train lomping down.

Just got out of the way in time.

Check the tracks, both ways.

Dark all round. And quiet suddenly, dead quiet. Not just my silence now. It's like the other sounds have faded. But they're still there, Bigeyes. You can hear 'em if you listen. See what I mean?

And that's what's weird. Cos before, you heard 'em automatic. Didn't have to try. But now we're down here, it's like they've faded. Only they haven't. They've never gone away. It's like you've gone away instead.

Freaks me out a bit.

OK, cut right. Yeah, you guessed it. We're heading under the bridge. Only it's not like with that little stream we went to. We're not going to rip a stone out of the wall. Watch close and you'll see.

Under the bridge, slow, slow. Could still trig into some duff we haven't seen. Or a druggie. Or some couple whamming. Looks cute though. On, on, under the bridge. That's right, Bigeyes. We're going all the way through and out again.

You're wondering why we didn't come down the other bank.

I'll show you.

Out the other side. Now then. Check right and left, top of the banks. See how high the fences are? Much higher than the one we climbed over. I'm telling you, the fences up there are a bogload of trouble to get over. Bank's steeper too.

So it's best to whip over where we did and cut under the bridge.

Anyway, we're nearly there. Up the bank, feeling with my hands. I can see the spot from here, Bigeyes, even in the darkness. Right by the side of the bridge, bushes clustered round, just down from the top.

Check out the fence. We're closer now. See what I mean? No one's going to try climbing that. Duffs and other nebs'll do what's easiest. Hit the other side of the bridge and stay there. They won't bother crabbing round here. Too much fuss.

Which makes this the perfect place.

Cos look.

Push through the bushes, scrabble under the roots and twigs and twisty branches, pull off the bits of broken rock. And there it is.

The old drain.

Just like I left it three years ago.

No water flowing through it now. Been blocked up for God knows how long and forgotten. By everyone except me. Cos it's not empty, Bigeyes, as you probably guessed. But like I said, we're not talking diamonds or jippy here.

Pull off the top, reach in, poke about.

And there's the familiar feel.

And the familiar feeling.

Don't know how to describe it, Bigeyes. Cos it's changed. Since Mary, Jaz, and all the stuff that's happened. It's different now. Used to be a kick, a buzz, a burst of something. Mixture of power and fear.

Now it's just the fear.

But it's still familiar.

And I got something else too. Something I didn't have before.

A reason.

Never had a reason before. Not a right one

anyway. So you better listen to this, Bigeyes. Look me in the face and listen good. Remember what I said to you? About tomorrow? I said keep your distance. Cos you won't like what I got to do.

Well, I won't like it either. But it's the only way.

Look down at the drain. Take a breath, pull 'em out.

Both knives.

Check 'em good, Bigeyes. Get used to 'em. Cos this is serious now.

Serious knives for serious work.

No flickies. These are heavy shit.

Go on. Look at 'em. Make yourself do it. And you might as well know. Both of 'em got a history. So here's the thing, Bigeyes. I'm being straight with you. So you know what's what.

Stay with me tomorrow if you want.

But if it bloods up, don't try and hold me back.

Or I'll turn these bastards on you.

OK, enough said. Hook the knives in my belt, pull the coat over 'em. Scramble down the bank, under the bridge, up to the fence, climb over.

Stop.

Listen again.

Gone quiet everywhere. Hear it? Silence all round. And now it's real silence. No traffic, no distant hum, nothing. But we're not the only ones listening.

He's listening too, Bigeyes.

The Beast.

Listening for me. My movements, my thoughts. And now I can hear him whispering, far off. Not here. It's still quiet in the Grinder. But far off, in his soul, he's calling me. And all his stinking minions.

Reach inside my coat, feel the knives.

Feel the feeling.

Whisper back.

'I'm coming.'

Drive, drive, out of the Grinder, into the night.

Sounds have started again. Sound of the engine, sound of other motors, shouts from the streets. Cos there's nebs out, young nebs mostly, cruising clubs, hitting pubs.

And still the Beast goes on whispering in my ear.

Calling, calling.

He doesn't need to. Cos I'm already heading back. But he goes on calling, like he's scared I might bottle out. But I won't. I'm choked up bad, but I'm in. I got the gig clear in my mind.

The Grinder's slipped away and I'm cutting for the centre. Cars hugging close, splash of lights all around. Drink him in, Bigeyes. The Beast's got a different face at night. Like the old city had. Difference is, she could be cute.

He can't.

He's got too much power. It's kind of an energy and it scares me. Cos it's out of control.

Got the old thoughts flooding now.

Becky, Mary, little Jaz.

And Bex. Even Bex.

Can't believe I'm worried about her, but I am. Don't suppose she's worried about me. Maybe she's phoned the police by now. Ruby's probably made her. I might not even get to the place I'm aiming for cos the porkers'll bang me up first.

We've passed three police cars on this road already.

Yeah, I know. You didn't see 'em.

Least one of us is awake.

Off the main road. I want to take some back streets. Got to play it cute to hit the spot I want. Right at the traffic lights, round the park, left at the junction. More shouts. Young nebs again, swilling from bottles.

Drive round 'em, checking good. I know the streets I want. Just a question of getting to 'em. Left, left again, on, on. And here's more young nebs. Blocking the way this time.

Black kids, gathered round something.

Think there's a fight going on. Yeah, I got it. Two trolls rolling on the ground, slamming each other. I can just see 'em. Can't get hooked into this. Check behind. No one pegging my bum. Reverse gear.

Thump!

Something crashes into the front of the car. Check round. Small rock rolling on the bonnet. Black kid further off, leering at me. Must have seen me, broken apart from the group and flung the rock.

He gives me the finger, turns back to watch the fight.

Squeal the car back, wheel round, race on. Rock

bumps off onto the street. Right at the junction. OK, Bigeyes, we're getting close. Keep your eyes open for porkers and grinks. And anything that looks dangerous.

Cos I got to tell you. It's getting hard now.

And tomorrow's going to be a tough shoot.

I got a plan, yeah, but success-wise we're talking fifty fifty.

At best.

There's a hundred things got to go right for this to work. And a hundred things could go wrong, easy. Most of 'em stuff I can't predict. It's hit and hope, Bigeyes.

And I'm scared.

Fifty fifty?

I was lying, talking it up. Truth is, that's a dream. We got nothing like fifty fifty. The odds are so bad I don't want to think about 'em.

But there is one good thing. I got the car sorted. I needed one for the plan but hadn't intended to jack a motor till later. Only problem is the porkers'll be looking for this one already.

And here's another problem.

Traffic lights on red and two porkers standing on the pavement.

Stop the car, check round. They're not looking my way. Too busy talking to each other. Just hope the lights turn green soon. Here they go.

Shit.

Car in front's stalled. Someone behind me blares a horn. Both porkers swivel round, check over the line of motors. Driver in front starts his car, stalls again. Tries a third time, revs up, moves off. But now the lights are changing back.

I'm not waiting.

Clutch up and go.

Both porkers fix me. I turn my head away, speed up. Halfway over the junction and now there's cars coming right and left, horns yamming. I drive on and over, and now I'm bouncing down the next street. Check the mirror.

Porkers staring after me.

One of 'em talking into his spinny.

Might not mean trouble. There's enough nebs who crash lights and they were only just changing when I went. Big problem is if the porkers check the registration number. They'll pick up it's a nicked car.

On, on. Right at the end, right again.

Got to crank up, Bigeyes, shift our stumps and put some distance between us and the police. Down the street, right at the end, and now watch good. We're cutting left, down this narrow lane.

Quiet little place.

High buildings either side. Check 'em out, Bigeyes. They're offices. Tired old offices. I know cos I've slept in a few of 'em. Easy to break into and most have got attics or storerooms for a doss. But we're not going there.

We're going here.

An even quieter place.

End of the lane, turn left, pull over.

Cut the engine.

How about that? Little cul de sac. And nobody in it. Warehouses on the left, garages on the right. Twelve in a row. Don't need to count 'em. I know there's twelve cos I've been here before. Lots of times.

Out of the car, close the door, check round.

Great spot this, Bigeyes, for all kinds of reasons. First up, we can't be seen. No problem with the warehouses. You're looking at the back of 'em. The nebs who work there are all on the other side. Nobody here anyway this time of night, and it won't be a problem tomorrow, unless we're very unlucky.

Other good thing is the garages.

There's always two or three empty. And even the ones that aren't don't get used much. Look at 'em. They're tatty as hell. I hardly ever saw anyone come here. And they're a whack to break into. Unless someone's dinked 'em up a bit.

But I don't think so. They look even more dronky than they did three years ago. And we only need one. Let's go. First garage.

Door's locked. Check the mechanism. No problem stinging that if I have to but we'll grub out the other garages first. There you go. What did I tell you? Second garage and we're jigging.

Door closes but the lock's broken, see? Open up, check round. Beautiful. Nothing in here but rusty tools and old paint pots. And almost no chance of the owner turning up.

First, he's not using it for his car. If he was, he wouldn't have the tools and pots all over the floor.

They'd be pushed to the side or the back. And second, I'm pretty sure he's not using the place for anything else.

Nothing in here except this junk. And look at it. The tools are old and crappy. Haven't been used for ages. And the paint pots are empty. No point looking any further. This'll do.

All I need is a place where I won't be disturbed. And I don't need it for long. Cos in less than a day, this thing'll be sorted, one way or the other. Reach down, shunt the tools and cans to the side. Straighten up, check round.

OK, Bigeyes.

I've found what I want.

Drive in, engine off, out of the car, pull down the garage door. Darkness closes around me. I stand there, breathing hard.

Distant sound of traffic. Only it's not so distant. There's cars and smellies and taxis only a short way off. They just sound distant, feel distant, and in the darkness they seem like they're from another world.

Look round, wait for my eyes to adjust. Takes a while, but I'm starting to see now. First time I've noticed there's a shelf on the far wall. Nothing on it but an old oil can.

Feel my breathing slow down.

I'm still standing, Bigeyes. Why'm I doing that? I got to rest, sleep, get ready for tomorrow. But I'm just . . . standing here, staring into the dark. What's wrong with me?

Edge round the car, slip into the driver's seat, close the door. Lock it. Don't know why I did that. Won't make any difference if they get inside the garage. Anyway . . .

Lean the seat back, far as it'll go. Take another breath. Close my eyes. Got to rest, Bigeyes. Got to sleep. Only I can't. All I see is more darkness. Inside my eyes, inside my head. And all the usual faces.

Becky, Mary, Jaz.

And now Bex and Ruby.

I'm so scared about tomorrow. Scared of what'll happen if it goes wrong. And scared of something else too. Myself. Yeah, I'm scared of myself. Open my eyes again.

Darkness is still there. Like it's never going to go away.

There's something I meant to tell you, Bigeyes. I lied to Bex. When I was talking about the network. She asked me if it's got a name, remember? And I said no. And that's true, sort of. Cos like I said, the grinks who get paid to sling the sludge don't get told much. They just carry out orders.

Right now they've been told to find a kid called Blade. When they've sorted him, they'll move on to the next job. And the spikes above 'em do the same. Carry out orders, move on.

None of 'em thinks about a name.

But there is a name, Bigeyes. A private name the slimeheads at the top use when they're talking about the operation. You know what they call it?

The Game.

That's right, Bigeyes.

The Game.

Cos to them, that's what this is. A huge, great game with massive stakes. We're talking power, politics, money, global change. That's what the grinks don't know, or the spikes. They just think they're cracking the usual criminal shit. They don't realize that the stuff they're doing is to finance something bigger.

Much bigger.

Cos the slimeheads are aiming high. I'm telling you, Bigeyes. The Game isn't about fun. Not to them. To them it's about life and death. The Game is all that matters. The Game is to be won. And they're very serious about winning it.

Yeah, yeah. You're wondering how I know.

Well, maybe one day I might just tell you.

But I got to get through tomorrow first.

I just wish I could sleep.

Jesus, Bigeyes, I'm so whipped up inside. I want to dash out, find a phone, ring The Crown, see if Mary's still alive, talk to her. And if she's not, ring Ruby. I know the number. I could talk to her. Or Bex, or . . .

Someone.

I just . . .

Want to talk.

And just for once . . . not be on my own when I'm feeling scared.

Sit up, fix the driver's seat upright, reach under my

coat. Pull out the knives. Hold 'em in front of me, blades up.

Didn't think I'd see these bastards again. Didn't want to either. Thought I could leave 'em behind, leave all knives behind. But it doesn't work that way, does it, Bigeyes? Not for me. Even when I throw 'em away, they come back.

But maybe I'm just zipping myself over.

I buried these two, didn't I? Didn't drop 'em in the water like I did that last one. I left 'em to be found again. And I chose to come looking. Maybe some part of me knew I was always coming back to the Beast. To face what I didn't finish when I ran away.

Picture of Jaz floats in front of me.

I swear I can see her. Her little face, staring at me, like it's hanging suspended inside the windscreen. Not smiling or anything. Just staring out, straight at me.

'I love you, baby,' I murmur.

She goes on staring. I whisper to her.

'I never finished that story. But I will, sweetheart. If you're still . . .'

I can't say it. Can't think it. I squeeze the two knives. And for a moment it looks like they're pointing

132

straight at Jaz's head. One each side. I drop my hands quick, stare back at Jaz's face.

But she's gone.

All I can see is the windscreen. I feel tears start inside me. I give a shudder, hold 'em in. I said I wouldn't cry. And I won't. Squeeze the knives tighter, climb out of the car, stand there. I don't know what to do, Bigeyes, and I can feel darkness closing round again.

Inside of the garage is fading.

Everything's fading.

I lean against the wall, slump down it to the floor, rest my head back against the brick. It smells of mould and I can feel a wisp of cobweb. Close my eyes again. And somehow I sleep.

Till a car horn wakes me.

I stiffen, sit up. I'm shaking and it takes me a moment to remember where I am. I feel drugged, cold, and I'm still frightened. Heart's pounding bad. Cos I can see through the gap at the bottom of the garage door. And it's morning. It's time to move.

Scramble up, stretch, breathe.

Think.

Keep to the plan, keep to the plan.

But get ready to change it. Cos anything can happen when the spit starts to fly.

I'm still holding the knives, Bigeyes, one in each hand. Put 'em away, out of sight. They're ready. And so am I. Just one more thing to find. Bound to be something I can use in this garage. Check among the old tools.

This'll do.

Small hammer. Light but strong. Hope I don't need it but best to have it in case. Stuff it in a pocket. Coat's bulging now, what with all the jippy as well. But I can't help that. I'm not leaving the money behind.

And I won't care about it anyway, if today goes bad.

Over to the garage door, listen. No sounds outside, apart from the early traffic humming round the Beast. Ease the door open, check out. Hard to tell what time it is. I'm guessing half six. Back to the car, check the clock.

Shit, it's ten past seven.

We got to shift.

We're much later than I meant to be. And there's stuff

to do before I hit the gig. Jump in the car, turn the key. Engine fires. Reverse out, close the garage door, back in the car.

Down the lane towards the main road.

OK, Bigeyes, we're going somewhere you've been before. When we get to the end of the road, check right. Hold on, wait. OK, look now.

Recognize that road?

Jesus, you don't, do you? Never mind.

Down the road, slow, steady. Got to stay legal, look normal. Lots of cars about already so we don't stand out too bad, but the porkers'll be looking for this motor. I only need it a bit longer so I'm hoping we'll be cute, but we still got to be careful.

OK, now look.

Left side of the road. See? That's where we hooked the taxi. And the grinks nearly closed us in. There's the allotment we ran through. That's right, Bigeyes.

We're coming back to the first place I showed you. The very first.

Up to the roundabout, second exit. Check right. See the turning? The little street? Me and Bex ran down that when the grinks found us in the alleyway.

And guess what. We're cutting down it again.

Right now.

You're thinking this is crazy, heading back to where they found us before. But I'll tell you something. It's no riskier than anywhere else in the Beast. And hopefully the grinks won't be expecting us here.

Down the street.

Recognize any of this? Bike sheds? Bank? Don't know why I bother asking. On, slow now, checking round. Pull over. OK, look left. Even you got to remember that.

Shoe shop. Little courtyard behind it. And behind that, the wall me and Bex climbed over from the alleyway. Don't panic. We're not climbing over it again. But we are getting out of the car. Cos I got to go to work. And I'm busted for time cos I slept too long. So we won't slap about.

Out of the car, check the street. Plenty of nebs already, as I expected. Pretty sure they're all muffins, but we got to watch cute. Hood back, beanie down. Walk slow, casual, side of the street.

Got to blend, OK? Stay out of sight. Used to be good at this. Still am but I've lost a bit of confidence.

And I'm so choked up with nerves right now I'm worried I might crash up. If there's grinks anywhere near, they'll smell that.

Walk on, end of the street, check round. Turn right, right again.

OK, Bigeyes, check the road in front of you. Go on. Now tell me you don't remember it. You got to. Alleyway down on the right, see? Where me and Bex hid. And over the road, the car park where the home used to be.

The one I burnt down.

Take a breath.

Walk to the jewellery shop, check through the window. Clocks all say different times but the one on the wall says half seven. Got to be right. Which case, I got to buzz on. Check round.

Loads of nebs on the street. Should be spoilt for choice. All I need's a mobile. I'd rather have two or three but I'll settle for one if I have to. Down the street, keeping back.

Woman climbing out of a car. Should be a whack. But I miss her. Old dunny slipping hers into her handbag. I miss that too. What's wrong with me? These are easy slams. But I can't crack 'em. I'm getting so choked I'm freezing up.

Two businessmen, trigging together. Neither holding mobiles. They're just naffing. I got to take a risk. Walk on, heading between 'em, face down like I'm not watching. Feel 'em break apart, step round me.

Walk on, wait, check behind. They haven't stopped.

Slope over to the side of the road, pull out the mobile. Looks OK. Switched on already and plenty of battery. Glance round. I could do with another one. Many as I can get really. Check the time on the mobile.

Quarter to eight.

Shit, I've wasted fifteen minutes on this.

Stomach's churning, Bigeyes. I got to go. Forget about more mobiles. Got to hit the car and blow blood. Back down the street, past the alleyway, stop at the end, check faces. Round the corner, left again, down towards the shoe shop.

Jesus!

Two police cars parked further down. Four porkers standing in the street.

Checking my motor.

Slip behind a dustbin.

I'm stuffed, Bigeyes. I can't do this without a car. And I'm never going to find one at this late stage. But I got to hook one. Got to sort this gig today. I've made up my mind. It can't wait any longer.

Back to the end of the street. I'm desperate now. Yeah, I'm still scared. But I was fired up for this and I still am. Round the block, down to the alley-way. Stop, look round. There's got to be something, Bigeyes. There's got to be. I can't wait another day. And it's not just cos of me. It's cos one more day could be too late.

Cars ripping past, left and right. Christ, Bigeyes, everybody's got a motor except me. Then I clap him. Over the road. In the car park. Where the home used to be. And I've seen him before.

The old gobbo in his ancient car. He had a boy with him last time, about four years old. Looked like his grandson. And there he is, in the passenger seat. They're getting out. Kid's running to the machine. Snaps the ticket, runs back. Gobbo's still heaving himself out of the car.

Got to go. Got to do this.

Over the road, into the car park. I'm pelting but I make myself slow down. If I freak 'em out, this won't work. Still might not cos I'm thinking bad and acting like a dimp. They've stuck the ticket on the windscreen and the old gobbo's locking the car.

Kid turns, sees me coming. Looks wary. I slow down to a walk, chuck him a smile. He doesn't look any happier. Bungs a glance at Grandad. The old gobbo turns, sees me.

'Good morning,' he says.

Still got the car keys in his hand. Gives me a smile.

'You look like you're in a hurry.'

Kid's still got that look on his face. It's putting me off.

I fix the old man, manage a smile back.

'Yeah, I'm a bit late. You couldn't tell me the time, could you?'

Gobbo slips the car keys in his pocket, glances at his watch.

'Ten to eight.'

I roll my eyes.

'Christ, I'm in trouble. Thanks a lot.'

I hurry forward.

'Good luck,' he says.

I slip past him, lift the keys from his pocket, walk on.

'Cheers, mate,' I call.

Keep walking, check over my shoulder. They're heading out of the car park. Gobbo looks relaxed. But the boy glances back one more time.

And then they're gone.

Back to the car, unlock it, jump in.

Heart's pounding again and I'm trembling bad. Check the clock. Seven minutes to eight. We're OK. We got time. Long as we don't get snagged with the traffic. Breathe slow, breathe slow. Got to calm down or I'll screw this gig.

Check round the car, make sure everything's cute.

Nice easy motor, nothing fancy. And look, Bigeyes. A little present.

He's left his mobile. Check it over. Jesus, what century did this thing come from? But it's switched on and I might need it. Pockets all bulging now but I shove it in.

Sit up, focus.

Take some more breaths.

Check I've got everything.

OK, OK.

And then suddenly it hits me. Something I wasn't ready for.

I'm fizzed up to go and in a couple more seconds I'll drive off and it'll start. But think for a moment, Bigeyes. Cos there's something else. I'm sitting on the site of the very place where everything started.

The home I first lived in.

The home that should never have been my home.

Or anyone else's.

And just for a moment, I feel it all again. Like I'm the same age as that boy who just bombed me with his look. I'm four years old again and I'm staring around me, and everything's burning, burning, burning.

Like I told you once before, Bigeyes.

Ghosts don't leave that easy.

Click on the belt, turn the key, rev up.

Out of the car park, into the road.

Down to the end, right at the lights. Speed steady. No

need to rush. Traffic's moving.

Here's the street. Turn down it.

Remember, Bigeyes? We came this way, right at the start. Check round. What do you see? Cars, yeah, but what kind of cars? What do you see when you really look at 'em?

Money.

That's what you see. In this street all you see is money. More cars, lots of 'em. All the same. Lovely cars. With lovely kids inside 'em. Rich kids.

Here's the school. Remember it? Course you do.

Pull over, stay back. Perfect spot. Clear view of the main gate. Lots of kids in the playground already and more spilling in. Check out all the nebs. The beautiful people with their beautiful children, rolling up in their beautiful cars.

And here's the one I want.

All discreet.

No need to crow about being the richest family here. Everybody knows it, specially at one of the most expensive schools in the world. So it's a low-key Merc, if there is such a thing, and it's driven by the nanny. And the two grinks in the car behind are low-key too.

Smart but not flash. Same gobbos as last time.

All discreet.

Can't believe how calm I've gone. Like all the tension's drained out now the gig's starting. But it won't be for long. Keep my eyes on the grinks. They're doing what they did last time. Keeping just behind.

But not too close. Everyone knows the boy in the Merc's got two bodyguards. But best not to upset the other parents. Cos some of 'em can't afford even one.

Yeah, grinks. Stay exactly where you are. Cos that's where I need you.

Fix the Merc. Two people in it. Damien and his nanny. She was better-looking in the old days. As for the boy . . .

I don't like watching him, Bigeyes.

He's six now but he was three when I ran away. Same age as Jaz is. And all I keep seeing is the face he had then. Only I can't bear to do it. Cos it's too much like hers.

Nanny pulls over. Grinks do the same just behind.

This is it.

I rev up, pull out, roar down the street, faster, faster.

Faces turn. Parents, teachers, kids, Nanny, Damien.

And now the grinks.

Both gobbos staring.

As I crash into the front of their car.

Shouts all around. My head's thumping. I braced myself ready for the impact but still got blammed. I kick the door open, stumble out of the car, blunder towards the Merc. Nanny and Damien are still in it, staring back at me. Nanny twists round, flicks on the central locking, revs up.

I grab the driver's door. Car starts to move off. I lose my grip, feel the car slip away. Grab the rear door, pull out the hammer, smash the glass, force up the lock. More shouts. Figures rushing close.

I yank the door open, throw myself into the back of the car, pull the door shut. Nanny slams on the brakes, screams at the boy.

'Get out the car! Get out the car!'

He doesn't move. He's frozen.

I whip out both knives, scramble between the front seats. Nanny tries to push me back but I thrust the blades at her face.

'Drive!' I bellow. 'Drive!'

She's not going to do it. She's staring at the blades, trying to hold out till help gets here. I see shadows close in on the car. I turn, dive on the boy, hold the knives over him. He screams. I bawl back at the woman.

'Drive or I'll cut him in two!'

She starts to drive, the boy still screaming under me.

'Faster!' I shout. 'Faster!'

She speeds up and now she's pulling clear. I check out the window. It's teachers giving chase and one of the grinks. His mate's sprawled over the steering wheel of their motor.

Check the distance between us. I've got seconds to get away. They'll hit the cars any moment. Glance at Nanny. She's shaking but she's holding up, and she's watching close, like she's trying to think what to do.

It's got to be now.

'Pull over,' I snarl.

She pulls over. I spring at her.

'No!' she screams.

I force the knives back at her face.

'Out the car!' I yell.

'No!'

'Out the bloody car!'

She's edging back. Doesn't want to, but I'm pricking the blades into her neck. I reach out, open the driver's door.

'Get out!'

'Don't hurt the boy!'

'Get out!'

I kick her in the thigh. She tumbles into the street and rolls over the ground. I slam the door, rev up, blast off, check the mirror. Four gobbos thundering in. I put my foot down, hard. They fall back and vanish behind.

Don't look at me like that, Bigeyes.

Don't look at me at all.

Drive on, fast as I can without drawing attention.

This is it. My chance. The only one I'll get.

Left at the traffic lights. Going to head the wrong way and cut back. Try and confuse anyone who sees me. Past the alleyway, past the car park, right at the end, on to the roundabout, right again.

And now I look at the boy.

Been avoiding it all this time.

Never mind why.

He's not looking back. He's curled up in a ball, hiding his face. Dark smelly patch round his trousers where he's peed himself. And I'm wondering, Bigeyes. Is that what Jaz was like? When they took her? Eh? ~~Got to keep wondering that. Keep remembering. Cos~~ that's the only way I'll get through this.

Down to the junction, right at the end, now back on myself. And here it is. The lane between the offices. Nobody in it like before. And I don't think anyone's clapped us cutting in. Down to the end, left, and here's the garages.

All deserted.

Glance at the boy. Still curled up, not looking at me.

And he's crying now, whimpering.

Out of the car, open the garage door, drive in, engine off. Close the garage door, back in the car. Breathe, slow. Look down.

Both knives sitting on my lap.

Did I put 'em there just now? Was I holding 'em when I opened the garage door? Can't remember. Suppose I must have been. And put 'em back again afterwards without thinking. I stare at 'em, hate 'em.

Pick 'em up.

Feel Damien stiffen and watch.

I look round at him, put the knives back on my lap. Pull out the mobiles. Which one? Both dronky. But hang on. There's a third choice. Nanny's left hers in the Merc. What could be better?

Pick it up.

I already know the private number. Told you once before, Bigeyes. I remember stuff. But I don't need to remember this one. Cos Nanny's got it listed in her phone.

Lord H.

That's what it says. How cute is that? Well, it's a long surname. I don't blame her keeping it simple. Take another breath. Stare down at the phone.

Lord H.

Select. Press Dial.

Rings only once. Like I knew it would. And here's the voice.

Quiet, familiar.

'Yes?'

I don't answer. Don't need to. He knows exactly who it is. And what I want.

Damien goes on whimpering. I reach out the mobile, hold it close to him, let the sound weep into the phone. And for a moment I see that face again. Jaz's face, hanging there, like it did last night. Staring at me. I stare back, watch it fade.

Till all I see is Damien again, sobbing.

I pull the phone back, raise it, listen.

Silence at the other end. A waiting silence.

It's time to break it.

'Let's talk,' I say.

tim bowler

BLADE

MIXING IT

In the next instalment of Blade . . .

He won't have changed at all. He'll be fifty-two
now but he'll still look like he's forty. Younger
even. An aristo god, master of all he surveys.
Blue eyes, sculptured cheeks, hair the colour
of a kiss.

If it wasn't for the mouth, you'd say it was
a kind face. And he can make it look kind when
he wants to, even with the mouth. He can make
it look anything. Only I know better. Cos I
know the face too well.

I hang up, drop the mobile on the floor, stamp
it to bits. Slump on the boards, wait. It won't
take long. They'll be here in minutes. And so will
he. That's right, Bigeyes. He'll come personally.
I know it. He'll be here in ten.

He's here in five.

I got my enemy. Got him fixed in my head. He was there before, course he was, but now I've seen him again, he's clearer than ever. And I know this for certain.

I can't run any more. You know why? Cos he'll never rest till he's found me. Till I'm dust trickling through his hands. So I got one choice left. Bring him down.

That's right, Bigeyes.

I got to mix it.

'Ruby,' I mutter, 'I know you hate me, but...'

It's no good, Bigeyes. The words won't come. I can feel 'em freezing in my mouth. I want to put things right, I swear I do, but talking's no good now. It's too late for that. Becky's dead and nothing'll bring her back.

Ruby speaks suddenly, grit-hard.

'I'll meet you.'

I stare back at Damien. He's watching me close again. And suddenly I see it, just for a moment, in those small, six-year-old eyes. The hawk, peering back.

Marking prey.

Though he doesn't know it yet.

Fern speaks again. And there's a shiver in her voice.

'They've got Jaz.'

Tim Bowler is one of the UK's most compelling and original writers for teenagers. He was born in Leigh-on-Sea in Essex and after studying Swedish at university, he worked in forestry, the timber trade, teaching and translating before becoming a full-time writer. He lives with his wife in a small village in Devon and his work-room is an old stone outhouse known to friends as 'Tim's Bolthole'.

Tim has written nine novels and won thirteen awards, including the prestigious Carnegie Medal for *River Boy*. His most recent novel is the gripping *Bloodchild* and his provocative new *BLADE* series is already being hailed as a groundbreaking work of fiction. He has been described by the *Sunday Telegraph* as 'the master of the psychological thriller' and by the *Independent* as 'one of the truly individual voices in British teenage fiction'.